Elise didn't think she'd ever get emotional over something as simple as a working shower, but when the spray came out in a steady stream, she whooped with excitement.

"I take it that we were successful," Harris said as he returned to the bathroom.

"Not *we*," Elise corrected him. *"You."*

"Yeah, but only because you power loaded me with the best coffee and pancakes in all of North Carolina."

"I've been a little out of practice. When I moved in with my aunt, she didn't allow any food she thought would be fattening. She was really big on appearances."

"For what it's worth," Harris's gaze leisurely traveled over her body, which was difficult to do since they were in such a tight space, "I think you look great just the way you are."

As soon as the first flicker of heat traveled from her neck to her face, Elise quickly bolted out of the tiny bathroom before she made a fool of herself.

Again.

Dear Reader,

I love participating in continuity series where several authors take part in forming individual books that all come together in the end. Like solving a puzzle, I'm given several pieces of information and then need to figure out the best way to assemble them all together. Sometimes those puzzle pieces take a lot of maneuvering and finessing before I can get them just right. This particular story, though, was easy to build since I had so many resources and personal experiences laying the foundation.

When I began writing *It Started with a Puppy*, I was in the middle of a massive home renovation following a devastating fire. Our house was still standing thankfully, but had to be gutted and stripped down to the studs. The before and after pictures they show you on those home renovation networks or in the glossy magazines don't always depict the reality of the in-between periods like the demolition mess, the unexpected delays, and the lack of hot water. And let me tell you, spending time in a construction zone is about the least romantic setting ever.

Yet romance usually finds us when we're least expecting it. In the latest installment of the Furever Yours series, hunky contractor Harris Vega and recently impoverished Elise Mackenzie aren't looking for anything more than a business partnership. Yet they can't help but find themselves battling both plumbing mishaps and their growing attraction as they work together to remodel homes and raise funds for a local animal shelter.

For more information on my other Harlequin Special Edition books, visit my website at christyjeffries.com, or chat with me on Twitter, Facebook and Instagram. I'd love to hear from you.

Enjoy,

Christy Jeffries

Twitter.com/ChristyJeffries
Facebook.com/AuthorChristyJeffries
Instagram.com/Christy_Jeffries/

It Started with a Puppy

CHRISTY JEFFRIES

Special thanks and acknowledgment are given to Christy Jeffries
for her contribution to the Furever Yours miniseries.

Recycling programs
for this product may
not exist in your area.

ISBN-13: 978-1-335-72410-6

It Started with a Puppy

For questions and comments about the quality of this book,
please contact us at CustomerService@Harlequin.com.

Harlequin Enterprises ULC
22 Adelaide St. West, 41st Floor
Toronto, Ontario M5H 4E3, Canada
www.Harlequin.com

Printed in U.S.A.

Christy Jeffries graduated from the University of California, Irvine, with a degree in criminology and received her Juris Doctor from California Western School of Law. But drafting court documents and working in law enforcement was merely an apprenticeship for her current career in the dynamic field of mommyhood and romance writing. She lives in Southern California with her patient husband, two energetic sons and one sassy grandmother. Follow her online at christyjeffries.com.

To Susan Litman, my favorite editor and enabler of all '80s and '90s pop culture references. I knew we were going to work well together the very first time I met you at a writers' conference in San Antonio. Of course, you weren't my editor yet, but you had a fabulous PowerPoint presentation and an even more fabulous purse, and that was all it took to convince me. Thank you for always laughing at my unrelated "side notes" in the margins and for always steering me in the right direction. I couldn't have built all those words without you.

Chapter One

Elise Mackenzie couldn't afford to be picky with her limited career choices, but at least she'd found a job working with animals rather than people. After all, dogs and cats didn't mind that she was better at making lists than making jokes, or that she talked to herself while she cleaned up after them. They didn't care how many followers she had on social media or that her nicest outfit was from the "unable to sell" bin at the rummage sale Aunt Regina organized for the church.

Scratch that.

Technically, Elise was the one who'd organized the rummage sale when it became clear her aunt had once again overvolunteered herself. Nobody would know that though because Elise preferred to remain behind the scenes and not draw any attention to herself. Her late mother had been the exact same way. Her father, on the other hand, used to joke that he was born with the gift of gab, a trait he unfortunately didn't pass down to his only heir.

"Pfshh," Elise sputtered as she hefted a twenty-pound bag of dry cat food from the back of her car. *Heir* made it sound as though she'd inherited some sort of vast estate or trust fund or anything besides a strong work ethic and this ancient minivan.

Elise had never had so much as a bank account until a week ago. As embarrassing as it was for a twenty-five-year-old woman to admit, working at Barkyard Boarding was her first official job and she'd just deposited her first real paycheck. Sure, Aunt Regina had begrudgingly given Elise a credit card to be used sparingly to pick up groceries for their household or her aunt's dry cleaning as needed. But when Elise moved out two weeks ago, she'd left the credit card on the counter in the kitchen.

Partly, she didn't want any ties connecting her to the town's most notorious socialite who'd mysteriously disappeared nearly a month ago and hadn't been heard from since. But more importantly, she needed to prove to herself—and to everyone else in Spring Forest, North Carolina—that Elise

Mackenzie could be her own woman and make her own way in this world.

Unfortunately, after deducting income taxes and paying her first month's rent, there was barely enough left over from her paycheck to buy groceries and cat food.

Still. Elise had never felt so in charge of her future.

Or at least she felt that way until a blue pickup truck pulled off Maple Street and into the driveway behind her van. Despite the warm September afternoon sunshine, a quiver made its way down her spine.

Harris Vega.

She nearly tripped over her own feet as she spun around and tried to focus on her original path. It's only Harris, she told herself. You've talked to him before. Sorta. He's just a man. And your new hot landlord. Not that he was recently hot. He'd always been that way. He was new to being her landlord, though.

And he was hot.

Gah, this was why Elise didn't like talking to people. She didn't want to risk accidentally voicing the random thoughts that popped into her head at the worst possible moments.

Without bending over and aiming her rear end in the direction of his truck, she tried to gracefully lower the awkward bag of cat food onto the worn boards of the bottom porch step. She lost her grip at the last minute and twenty pounds of kibble landed with a loud thunk, sending up a cloud of dust to tickle her nose. Maybe if she had a sneeze attack, Harris wouldn't notice the overgrown weeds in the front yard. Or that the front porch still didn't have so much as a doormat, let alone a fresh coat of paint.

Why was he here? Had he heard that she'd just cashed her first check and now he was rethinking his recent offer to forego the security deposit and full rent in exchange for her cleaning up the rental house and doing some minor renovations?

She had to come up with something to distract him. But as she turned toward the driveway to greet him, she couldn't muster so much as a sniffle. Probably because Elise purposely trained herself to blend into the background whenever possible and to avoid anything that might get her noticed.

Harris walked toward her with his brilliant smile and athletically lean six-foot-tall frame. His dark brown hair and sun-bronzed complexion might've been courtesy of his Mexican American heritage, but his well-worn work jeans and his easy stride likely came from an earned confidence of being one of the most successful contractors—and best-looking men—in Spring Forest. Elise's throat got so tight, all she could manage was a half-hearted wave hello.

"I see you already beat me to it," he said, and she knew he wasn't talking about the end-of-summer weeding that was just one of many items on Elise's long to-do list.

"Beat you to what?" Her voice sounded faint, as though it hadn't been used all day.

He nodded toward the toppled sack on the porch. "To feeding the cats. I bought the exact same bag of food. I don't know who came up with the name Feline Finest, but the former owner said it was the only brand her precious babies would eat."

"Oh." The tension in Elise's neck loosened with relief. "Right. Mrs. O'Malley sent me a letter saying the same thing. She even included a coupon."

"Lucky you. I paid full price. I tried to tell her that a colony of feral cats would be happy with anything I put in front of them, but she refused to move into the retirement home unless I promised I'd only buy them Feline Finest."

Elise watched as he walked to the bed of his truck and easily hefted an identical twenty-pound bag onto one of his shoulders. With his arm raised over his head to hold the awkward load securely in place, the hem of his work shirt rose as well, exposing the lower ab muscles just above his narrow waistband. She quickly looked away before he could catch her staring at him the way Roscoe, the Saint Bernard staying the week at Barkyard Boarding, stared at the container of treats he knew Elise kept at the reception desk.

"So I guess old Mrs. O'Malley made us both promise the same thing."

Elise shook her head to clear it. "I'm sorry. What?"

"I said, I'm guessing you also promised Mrs. O'Malley that you would feed the cats who roam around the neighborhood looking for a free meal."

"I didn't really promise her. I just noticed them hanging around behind the back fence in the evenings. When I sent her a letter, I asked about them."

"Really?" His light brown eyes opened wider. "I didn't know you and Mrs. O'Malley were pen pals."

Elise nervously bit her lip to keep from replying that there were plenty of things Harris Vega didn't know about her. "Actually, I've never met her, but when I was cleaning out the dining room hutch, there were some old photos that looked important, so I asked the postal carrier if they had a forwarding address. I found out she'd moved to Horizons Memory Center. That was the same place where my father went when he started having issues that made it difficult for him to live on his own. I remember he had such a hard time adjusting to the change, so I thought she might enjoy a little note to brighten her day."

Harris tilted his head as he studied her so intently, she began to wonder if he was staring at something in the overgrown hydrangea bushes behind her. But the only thing threatening the thick green leaves was the canvas sneaker on her right foot as she took another step back.

No, she decided before stiffening her shoulders and planting her feet. She was trying to be more independent. Less awkward. More capable of doing things like talking with hot guys without tripping over her feet or her tongue. After all, it wasn't as though the man standing before her was a complete stranger. They weren't exactly friends, but they knew some of the same people and Harris was a respected member of the community. He'd also given her a pretty big break on the rent when most people would've asked for a list of references and full credit report.

Unfortunately, it had been a long time since someone had looked at Elise the way Harris was looking at her now. Studying her with unabashed curiosity.

To keep from squirming under his direct stare, she cleared her throat and began walking toward the more accessible back door. "So do you want to see what I've done so far with the house? I haven't gotten to everything on the outside, obviously, but I was able to get that musty turquoise carpet pulled out of both bedrooms. The hardwood floors underneath are heart pine and in surprisingly good condition for being original to the house. They need to be sanded of course and restained. But I'll have to rent an electric sander from the hardware store, which will have to wait until I get my next paycheck. I did get some paint samples for the walls, though. But I didn't know if you wanted me to get your approval or if I should just go with my choice—Moonlight Serenade. The name is a bit over-the-top, but it's a pretty neutral tone and will go with most decor schemes in case the next resident prefers something…"

Elise paused long enough to push a stray bit of hair from her face. She'd been so busy rambling on and on to steady her nerves, she'd barely noticed whether Harris had followed her around the side of the house. He had, though, and his curious expression was now accompanied by a wide grin. Why was he smiling at her like that?

"The next resident? Are you already planning on moving out?"

"No! I mean. I was just thinking that eventually you'll want to sell the place and…" she trailed off again. Why couldn't she finish a damn sentence when he was watching her so intently?

"Oh, I don't think I'll be ready to sell this place anytime soon. Especially if it gets overrun with all the wild cats both of us are planning on feeding."

This time it was Elise who tilted her head and studied him.

She'd grown so accustomed to her aunt overcommitting and not following through, her brain was struggling to process the fact that Harris was actually making good on his promise to a little old lady who would probably never know whether or not he fed a bunch of strays.

Of course, she shouldn't be so surprised since she was about to do the same thing despite having never made an offer in the first place. But Elise had been raised by her parents to do what she could to help others. She hadn't imagined anyone would know about her care of the cats other than the cats themselves. But now here was Harris Vega.

She gestured at the heavy bag of food still balanced on his shoulder, trying to avoid looking at any other part of his well-formed torso. "Um, I did a bit of research online, but did Mrs. O'Malley give you any specific instructions on how to go about this? Or how often?"

"She said three evenings a week. Any more than that and they'll get too dependent and slowly forget their natural predatory skills. One of Mrs. O'Malley's friends was initially helping with the feedings, but I just found out he's in the hospital. I'm not sure when he was here last."

"Oh, how terrible. Let's hope the cats' predatory skills are nicely honed by now since I've been living here for a whole week and as far as I know, nobody has fed them yet."

A loud meow sounded from beyond the fence.

It was soon followed by another. Harris shifted the bag to his other shoulder, causing the bits of kibble inside to rustle loudly. A gray Bengal jumped up onto the fence post, balancing agilely on all four paws.

"I think they just heard the dinner bell," he said before tugging on his collar. Harris's smile was now replaced with a concerned frown. "Do you know how many of them are over there?"

"I'm sure there can't be that many," Elise tried to reassure him. Unfortunately, several more meows drowned out her response. She raised her voice so he could hear her over the growing howls. "Maybe they're just extra hungry because it's been so long."

"That's what I'm afraid of. What if I go over there and they mistake *me* for the food?"

She had to choke back a giggle. Surely, this normally confident and visibly strong man couldn't be afraid of a couple of small cats.

"Please. I'm sure you're not *that* yummy." It wasn't until Harris cocked an eyebrow at her that she realized what she'd just said. Heat rushed to her cheeks. "I mean... Not that I would know what you taste like."

His gaze lowered to her mouth and she instinctively bit her lower lip. Was it her imagination or did his eyes narrow? If she didn't know better, she'd think Harris Vega was actually considering the thought of her finding out for herself exactly how yummy he was.

"I have a feeling the defenses are about to be breached," Harris said without taking his eyes off Elise. It took her a few seconds to realize he wasn't talking about the emotional wall she'd spent years building up.

He was talking about the dilapidated backyard fence that wasn't stable enough to hold the weight of so many hungry cats.

"Do you have some scissors or something nearby?" Harris yelled over the growing cacophony of meows. "It'll probably be safer to just cut the bag open and throw it through the gate."

"I have a pair in the house," Elise replied. "But I don't know if the starving masses will be willing to wait that long. It could be risky."

Harris suddenly wondered if the timid young woman was actually cracking a joke. Unfortunately, he couldn't read her expression because he was too busy keeping his eyes locked on the feline army assembling before him. "Okay. I have a pocketknife on my keychain in my left pocket. I can't reach it with my free hand, and I don't want to make any sudden movements. Can you grab it for me?"

"You mean you want me to, uh…um…retrieve it?" There was a catch in Elise's voice, suggesting her cheeks had turned that charming shade of pink again. "From your pocket?"

"I promise I'm not trying to put the moves on you or anything." His new tenant had just spoken more words to him in the past few minutes than he'd heard from her, total, since he'd first met her. The last thing Harris wanted to do was scare the woman off. Especially since he might need someone to drive him to get a rabies shot after this.

He thought he might've heard her say, "Why would I ever think that?" But her normally soft tone wasn't quite audible with all the howling going on around them.

He caught a faint scent of lavender as though she'd moved closer toward him, but his pocket remained untouched. Even if he wanted to turn his head to find out what was taking her so long, he wouldn't have been able to see over the bag balanced on his shoulder. If he wasn't in such a damn hurry, Harris might have enjoyed her slow approach and the potential for some harmless flirtation with the shy, yet pretty woman.

He imagined her reaching for his pocket, then pulling her hand back as though she was about to get burned. He clenched his jaw, trying not to anticipate the moment her fingers would finally come into contact with his front hip. By the time he felt a slight tug on his jeans, he nearly jumped.

And so did the stealthy gray Bengal, who was now on the grass ten feet in front on them.

"Hold still or else he'll sense your fear," Elise whispered as her hand slowly slid inside his pocket. Harris held his breath, wishing he could explain that his jumpiness was a result of her touch, not his fear of some wild and possibly rabid animals who were visibly stalking him as though he was human catnip. "Feral cats aren't used to interacting with humans."

"Do you think we should maybe stop using the word *feral*?" He sucked in a gulp of air as the key ring—or possibly her fingers—grazed along the thin fabric separating his pocket from his skin. "I mean, ol' Mrs. O'Malley was about ninety-five pounds soaking wet and she was never attacked. Right?"

But Elise didn't answer. She'd already pulled his pocketknife free and handily used the blade to stab into the bag of food, slicing a long clean line only inches away from his left ear.

"Oh, so *now* you're in a hurry?" He didn't think he could hold his body any stiffer. "If you cut me, those beasts are gonna smell fresh blood."

"Don't worry. I have more experience using a knife than I do reaching into men's pants."

This time, Harris did jerk his head toward her and was rewarded with another view of her blush-stained cheeks. "Don't think I'm not going to ask you more about that later. If we make it out of here alive."

"I'm more likely to die from embarrassment than you are from some hungry cats." Elise deftly closed the blade and slipped the key ring into her own pocket. "On the count of three, I'll run and open the gate and then you can throw the food in their direction. Ready?"

Harris didn't know if the blood pulsing through his body was from his heightened adrenaline or from the unexpected rush of witnessing the very quiet and demure Elise Mackenzie take charge. Yet before the telltale blush was gone from her cheeks, she'd already called out "three" and was running toward the gate.

Harris had no choice but to act now.

He heaved the bag through the narrow opening and it landed with a loud thud, the freshly sliced tear causing some of the food to spill out. Four cats walked closer to inspect the bag, but none of them attacked it the way he expected.

"Why aren't they eating?" Elise asked.

"I have no idea."

She pointed to three short metal troughs that were spaced a few feet apart. "Maybe they're waiting for us to put the food in those things?"

"Seriously? After a week of not being fed? I've seen house cats not trained that well. These guys are feral."

"I thought we weren't using that word anymore." Elise pushed a wavy curl from her face. It was the second time she'd done that, and Harris had a sudden urge to see what she would look like with her hair down.

He cleared his throat. "Well, now that they're not attacking me, I'm comfortable putting it back into our vocabulary."

He thought she might've giggled, but if she had, it was short-lived. "Look, there's a big scoop attached to that bin. Clearly, Mrs. O'Malley had these feeding stations all set up for a reason."

Harris stepped closer to the open bag that the cats still hadn't touched. The meows grew more intense and several of the cats began actively pacing, but not even one touched so much as a single bite of kibble.

Nor did they attack him.

He swiped a hand against the back of his damp neck. So maybe he'd slightly overreacted earlier, but how was he supposed to know what to expect? One darted between his work boots, and when he took a step back, he nearly tripped over another. There were at least eight strays back here. If they decided to work together, they could possibly take down a human.

Elise retrieved the scoop and the cats immediately vanished from under Harris's feet and ran to the little feeding stations. It reminded him of visiting his tia Sylvia in Mexico when he was a kid. She would make homemade churros and he and his cousins would line up like patient little soldiers waiting to get handed one freshly dipped in cinnamon and sugar.

"How much do you think I should feed them?" Elise asked.

Harris shrugged. "I have no idea. I guess just put a few scoops out to see what they do. We don't want them to overeat. Is that a thing?"

"Right now, we have a twenty-pound calico at Barkyard Boarding who would eat in his sleep if we let him."

"You mean Mr. Chow's cat Dimples? I thought that thing was a potbellied pig the first time I saw it. Wait. Here come a few more." Harris began counting aloud. "I can't believe Mrs. O'Malley used to do this three times a week. How did she even manage to carry the food back here?"

"My guess would be that wheelbarrow parked over there, holding up this side of the fence." Elise went to retrieve it and his eyes were drawn to the way her jeans clung to her thin, but toned legs.

Watching her navigate the cumbersome bucket of rust made him realize he'd underestimated the woman. She was slim, but strong. Shy, but not afraid to take charge. He needed to remind himself that she was his tenant and he shouldn't be having those kinds of thoughts about someone who was paying him rent. "Yeah, maybe your landlord will get around to fixing that fence one of these days."

Her answering smile fled when the front tire of the wheelbarrow hit a rut and the axel broke. "Looks like I need to add a few things to my hardware store list."

"Yeah, but I don't want you paying for those kinds of things yourself." Harris wasn't sure what her financial situation was, but it couldn't be good. Not after her aunt had skipped town under questionable circumstances. "I have an account at the hardware store. Have the manager bill whatever you buy for the house to my company."

She opened and closed her mouth several times before finally saying, "Thanks. That'd be great."

Just like the day he'd offered to rent the Maple Street property to her for a reduced price, Elise turned away before he could read her emotions. Which was probably for the best.

When she finished refilling all three feeding stations, there was still more than half of the bag left. He dumped the remaining food into a steel bin with an airtight lid and a series of tricky latches that even the wiliest critter couldn't bust open. Then he did some quick calculations in his head.

It looked like one bag of food would only cover a week of feeding. And these strays had expensive tastes. He didn't want to keep bringing up money, but it didn't seem fair for her to use her own financial resources to keep a promise that Harris had made. At the same time, he looked at his watch and realized how long this visit had taken. His business couldn't afford for him to be over here three times a week feeding a bunch of strays either.

When Elise put the scoop back into its holder on the side of the bin, Harris asked, "So how would you feel about a little partnership?"

She whipped her head around, as though she thought he was talking to someone else behind her. When she realized he was talking to her, she asked, "What do you mean?"

"Well, to be honest, when I made my promise to Mrs. O'Malley, my business was running at full staff and I thought her friend would be helping out. But I'm currently down four guys and I've got two houses closing escrow this week, plus a big demo starting in a few days. Mrs. O'Malley's friend is getting discharged from the hospital this week, thank God, but he is going to be on bed rest for a while."

"Oh, I'd be happy to help." Elise wiped her hands on the denim outlining the curve of her hips. "I'm used to being on the cleanup crew."

Harris had been so focused on her legs, he'd only caught the last bit of what she'd said and wasn't sure he'd understood. He shook his head to clear it. "Please tell me you're not saying there's a bunch of litter boxes around here we have to deal with too."

She chuckled, which was more of a hiccup coupled with a smile, but Harris realized he'd never seen her laugh before. "No litter boxes, thank goodness. The cleanup crew was a reference to Aunt Regina. She also tends to bite off more than she can chew when it comes to volunteering. It was my job to make sure nothing fell through the cracks."

Harris felt as though a twenty-pound bag of Feline Finest had just been dropped on his stomach. Everyone in Spring Forest knew that Regina Mackenzie was a notorious flake. She ran in much higher social circles than he did, or at least she used to before she vanished off the face of the earth under unscrupulous circumstances. He hoped Elise wasn't seriously comparing him to *that* Aunt Regina.

To keep from scrunching his nose in disgust, he dragged a hand across the lower half of his face, which was covered with a bit more stubble than his mom approved of.

"It's not that I can't handle doing the feedings. I can." Even though he clearly couldn't handle shaving more than once or twice a week. "I would just need to switch some stuff around in my schedule. I can't always promise that I'd be here at a specific time, and I wouldn't want to bother you if you had plans or were entertaining someone."

Her eyebrows drew into a V over her narrow nose. "Who would I be entertaining?"

"I don't know. Maybe a guy. Or a friend. Or a

guy friend." Great. Now he sounded as though he was asking her if she had a boyfriend. "Anyway, I wouldn't want to be showing up at random times and…" he trailed off when he felt her palm on his bicep.

"Harris, I really am happy to help. There's no point in you driving out all this way from…wherever you live when I'm already here. Besides, you've already cut my rent in half in exchange for working on the house and yard. Let's just put this under that same umbrella. Taking care of the cats is part of taking care of the property. Think of this as basic maintenance."

"Fine. But I pay for the food. And you call me immediately if you need me to take over in case you can't handle it. Or if you run into a problem."

Elise stared at him, and he wished he knew what she was thinking in that moment. He almost asked and then her gaze shot past him, to something in the distance. He followed her line of sight.

Harris spotted the skinny orange tabby hovering near a fir tree and asked, "Why isn't that one eating with the others?"

"That's what I'm trying to figure out. It looks like it could use a good meal."

"Maybe he's afraid of the other cats."

"Possibly. But it doesn't seem as though they're paying any attention to him. He could be afraid of you."

"Of me?" Harris's voice came out much louder than he'd intended. "What did I do to make him afraid?"

"Shhh. Some animals are afraid of big men."

"I'm not that big." Harris couldn't help the pride causing his shoulders to straighten wider. "Besides, how do you know it's not *you* scaring him away?"

"I don't scare anybody," Elise said as she took a tentative step toward the orange tabby. "In fact, people usually don't even know I'm there."

The cat ducked behind the tree. "Looks to me like he knows exactly where you are, and he doesn't want you to come any closer."

"I think that's Oliver. The cat Brooklyn Hobbs has been searching for." In fact, the nine-year-old had posted signs all over town and even went to the shelter every week to see if someone had found her missing cat.

"He looks a lot thinner than his picture on the flyer, but I think you're right," Harris said, full of relief. The whole town had been pulling for the owner and pet to be reunited, but with all the time that had gone by, it had started to seem less and less likely. "I'll go get him." Harris took several long strides before Elise grabbed his hand and tugged him back.

"Don't startle him. You need a plan first."

He looked down at their joined fingers. "My plan is to go after what I want."

Chapter Two

Again, Elise felt her cheeks burning, and she instinctively yanked her hand away. Relax, she told herself. It wasn't as though Harris was saying that *she* was what he wanted.

"Unless you want to climb up that tree," she said as calmly as she could manage, "you might need to come up with a more practical approach. Do you have any cat treats on you?"

"Like in my pocket?" Harris asked and Elise had to suppress the memory of how she'd had to intimately navigate the inner lining of his pants when she was retrieving his pocketknife earlier.

"Or in your truck."

"All I have in there is a half-eaten protein bar and a bottle of warm Gatorade. Oh, and a bag of dill pickle–flavored sunflower seeds."

"Dill pickle–flavored?" Elise wrinkled her nose. "Even the squirrels wouldn't touch those. Okay, I think there's a can of tuna in the kitchen pantry. If I run back to the house to get it, promise me you won't do anything to scare off Oliver while I'm gone."

She didn't wait for his assurance before sprinting all the way to the back porch. All she could think of was little Brooklyn Hobbs and how anxious the poor girl was to have her cat home. Many of the pantry items Mrs. O'Malley left behind had expired, but the tuna might still be okay. Elise had thrown most of the other stuff out when she'd done a deep clean on the kitchen but was now relieved she held back a few things. Even though it seemed kind of desperate to eat an old woman's food after she moved out, there were a couple of times last week when Elise didn't have any extra money to waste on groceries.

She grabbed the tin can now and sprinted back, using the metal ring to pop open the top as she ran. Big mistake. The liquid contents splashed all over her neck and the front of her shirt.

Thankfully, many of the strays had eaten their fill and already left for parts unknown. From the limited research she'd done, cats that were truly feral preferred not to interact with humans at all. She should've reassured Harris of that fact earlier when he'd seemed spooked that the animals might attack him. But she already felt at such a disadvantage around the handsome, successful man, it was kind of nice to have the upper hand, even in a small way.

After he'd made her blush several times, Elise would take whatever advantages she could get. Then there was that whole *if you run into a problem* comment he made. He likely didn't mean to offend her, but it sounded like a polite way for Harris to say he expected Elise to be inept.

When she got back to the feeding stations, Harris was standing in the exact spot where she'd left him. But the orange tabby was gone. Elise scanned the area. "Where'd he go?"

Harris shrugged. "All I did was take three or four steps. Ten at the most. And he was up the tree before I could stop him. I came back over here to wait him out."

Clearly, Harris Vega really did go after what he wanted. Even if it ended up costing him in the long run. Elise rolled her eyes. Lord save her from impulsive people. "Maybe you should go stand over there by the gate while I try to lure him down."

"With an empty container?" Harris didn't look convinced.

Elise glanced down to see that it hadn't just been

the liquid sloshing out of the can. All the meat was gone too. Crap.

"I'll just go back to the yard and find a piece…" She stopped talking as she saw the gray Bengal quickly making its way along a trail of spilled tuna, gobbling up every last piece. She took a deep breath and sighed. "Well, we might have to try the protein bar in your truck after all."

"Or, uh…" Harris was staring at the spot where the third button of her blouse used to be. "We could use that."

Elise lowered her head and saw a chunk of tuna stuck directly in between her breasts, the center clasp of her bra preventing it from sliding all the way down her shirt.

Gasping, she used one hand to dive for the piece of fish while using the other hand to clench the fabric together. She vowed to never try her hand at sewing buttons again, no matter how cute she thought something was in the secondhand store.

Harris's lips were twitching as though he was struggling to hold back his laughter. "Here, I'll take it over to him so you can see to your…uh…top."

Mortification flooded Elise's body, urging her to race right back into the house to change into something that covered her all the way up to her chin. But she wanted to catch the missing cat more. And if she left their last piece of bribery tuna to Mr.

Goes-After-What-He-Wants, then Brooklyn Hobbs might not ever see her beloved Oliver again.

"I'll just sit here." Keeping the edges of her shirt together, Elise awkwardly lowered herself to a cross-legged position and extended one arm. "And hold it out like this. When he gets close enough, you *gently* scoop him up."

Harris nodded, then lifted his head toward the tree. "He's looking this way right now."

"Don't make any sudden movements. We need to wait him out."

A minute passed. And then five minutes. Harris rocked back on his heels and checked his watch at least a hundred times. Elise's arm was starting to get tired. Oliver tentatively jumped to a lower tree branch.

Harris took a step forward. "I think I can reach him—"

"Don't you dare move," Elise whispered so forcefully, it sounded like a hiss. "Sit down here next to me, so you don't seem like a threat."

"Don't move or sit down? I can't do both, Lise."

Lise. Nobody had ever called her by a nickname and the unexpected familiarity of it sent a wave of warmth through her. This time, her voice was softer when she whispered, "Sit."

The man was quick, yet agile as he knelt beside her. He was close enough that the musky scent of his soap almost covered up the unfortunate odor of tuna now emanating off her. Almost.

Another look at his watch. "I don't think he's going to come down."

"He'll come down. We have to be patient."

"Did I mention that patience isn't exactly in my wheelhouse?"

"You didn't have to." Elise couldn't hold back her smile. But when Harris didn't say anything else, she took her eyes off the cat in the tree long enough to sneak a peek at what he was doing.

That was her second big mistake of the day. Or maybe the fortieth. Elise had lost track of how many she'd made so far. But catching Harris Vega staring at her had to be in the top five.

Her heart beat a fast tempo against the knuckles that were keeping her shirt together. For a second, Elise had the fleeting thought of releasing her shirt, just to see what he would do. But then she immediately regained control of her runaway brain.

"You're supposed to be watching for the cat," she reminded both of them.

Harris looked away quickly but didn't deny that he'd been actively studying her. Instead he lowered his voice. "Here he comes. No, don't make eye contact with him. Keep looking at me. That's it. He's almost here. Hold still. Let him sniff your hand. I'll wait until he eats before I pick him up."

"Please let this work," Elise whispered, holding

as still as she possibly could while the cat took its first tentative bite. As soon as Oliver gulped down the rest of the chunk of tuna, Harris easily—and surprisingly gently—scooped the animal into his arms.

Oliver meowed, and his paws stretched open, but he didn't make a move to fight. Harris murmured reassurances to the terrified cat until the claws retracted. Then he slowly stood. "I think he's still hungry. Do you have any more tuna down your shirt?"

Elise wasn't about to expose herself again to check. At least not while Harris was watching. "No, but we can give him some dry food from the feeders."

"I don't think I should let go of him. Maybe we can put some food in the carrier with him."

"Did you bring a carrier?" she asked.

"No, I was hoping there was already one out here."

Elise scanned the feeding stations and the dense pine trees surrounding them. "There might be some sort of cage buried in the shed beside the carport, but Mrs. O'Malley was a bit of a hoarder and I haven't had enough spare time to go through everything yet. If there *was* one in there, it would take forever to find."

"Okay. The animal shelter isn't that far from

here. I'll drive and you hold Oliver so he doesn't freak out in the truck."

Elise's whole body went heavy, her feet became slow and reluctant as she followed Harris and Oliver across the yard and toward the driveway. She'd started volunteering at the shelter after her dad passed away, taking solace in the sweet animals who didn't really fit in anywhere either. However, this would be her first time going to Furever Paws since Aunt Regina left town right after promising to host their fundraiser. What would the owners, Bunny and Birdie Whitaker, say when they saw her?

Don't think about that, she resolved as she commanded her legs to move faster. Focus on what Brooklyn Hobbs will say when she sees her lost cat.

Harris stopped by the passenger side of his truck holding a somewhat calmer, but still wide-eyed Oliver. "I would get the door for you, but I don't want to risk losing my grip on him."

When was the last time anyone—let alone a man—had held open a door for Elise? Probably not since she'd dated… No. This was *not* a date. She tugged on the handle a bit too hard, nearly throwing herself off balance before she climbed inside. That was when she realized his keys were still in her pocket. She lifted her hips to yank them free and heard Harris clear his throat. His voice was slightly lower when he said, "Just toss them on the center console."

Someone above must've thought she'd experienced enough embarrassment today already because when she got the seat belt in place, she discovered that it held the top of her blouse together so she could use both hands to take a squirming Oliver from Harris.

The cat immediately relaxed in her arms—or at least he did until Harris started the engine and loud music blasted out of the speakers. His hand shot toward the volume button, but not before Elise realized what song it was.

"Were you listening to the cast recording from *Hamilton*?"

This time, it was Harris's cheeks that seemed a bit flushed. Although it was hard to tell under the black stubble of his five o'clock shadow. "I might have a few of the songs on my playlist. My mom was a drama teacher and raised me to appreciate the theater."

"Were you ever in any plays?"

"I auditioned for a few school productions when I was a kid, but never got cast. This might surprise you, but I had a little trouble waiting for my cue and always said my lines too fast."

Elise's head shot back as she laughed, startling both Harris and Oliver. When neither male would stop staring at her, she sat up straighter and said, "We should probably get going."

They were already backing out of the driveway when the hungry cat sniffed out the lingering tuna smell on her chest and shirt. They were turning off Maple Street when Elise squeaked, "Oh no."

"What's wrong?" Harris asked as he drove a few miles over the speed limit.

"We…uh…forgot to bring the dry food."

Now it was Harris holding back a chuckle as Oliver nudged his tiny nose under the seat belt, nosing aside the collar of her shirt to try to "clean" the remnants of tuna juice from Elise's skin.

"Stop laughing," she told Harris. "This is very uncomfortable."

"But look at how calm he's being. I'd be purring like that too if I—"

"Hey, Oliver," Elise interrupted before Harris said something that might embarrass them both. She grabbed a small bag off the center console and shook the contents into her palm. "Wanna try some sunflower seeds? They supposedly taste like dill pickles."

The cat briefly sniffed at her offering and then used a paw to push her hand away. Harris chuckled. "No offense taken, little guy. The flavor's not for everyone."

At least she no longer had to hold the nervous animal. He'd thankfully found a wet spot on the outside of her blouse to focus his attention and was in no hurry to get away. Pulling onto the highway, they passed another one of Brooklyn Hobbs's lost cat flyers taped to a streetlight. Elise sighed, realizing she had no choice but to let Oliver lick her shirt if she wanted to keep him from becoming overly skittish before they got to the shelter. "At least we found you, little guy. Maybe we should post some missing pictures for Aunt Regina next."

"Does your aunt normally take off like this?" Harris asked, making her wish she'd kept her thoughts to herself.

Too late now. After nearly a month of no word from the woman, people were already starting to wonder what was going on.

But that didn't mean Elise couldn't avert her gaze out the window as she spoke. "There've been times when she'd leave unexpectedly and come back a week or two later with a car full of shopping bags or a fresh cosmetic procedure. She used to refer to it as recharging her batteries. But she's never been gone this long. I went to the Spring Forest Police Department thinking I should possibly file a missing persons report. But since she took a suitcase and drove off in her own car, it looks like she left town of her own free will, for whatever reason."

She chanced a look in Harris's direction just in time to see him open his mouth, then immediately snap it shut. He must have an opinion about why Aunt Regina left. But before she could ask him to tell her, they pulled into the parking lot at Furever Paws.

When they went into the shelter, Elise was the only one Oliver would allow to hold him. Which was fine with Harris. Tomorrow, he was scheduled to strip about seven layers of lead paint from the banister at the old Cooper house and he didn't want to deal with a bunch of open wounds from cat scratches when he was handling toxic chemicals.

The volunteer at the front desk immediately used the microchip scanner to verify that this was indeed Brooklyn Hobbs's missing cat. But Oliver used his claws to cling to Elise's shirt, his eyes wide with terror.

"The poor guy has probably been through so much these past months," the volunteer said. "The vet is going to want to examine him, but all of our techs already left for the day. Would you guys mind keeping him calm while I call the Hobbs family?"

And that's how Harris ended up sitting next to Elise and a very skittish Oliver in the exam room, thinking of all the job plans requiring his attention when the veterinarian walked in grinning. "I hear you two rescuers are about to make a certain little girl very, very happy."

"Doc J, I didn't know you were back in town."

Harris stood up to shake the doctor's hand. He'd always liked the retired vet, who had a beautifully restored Victorian house he'd put on the market when he moved to Florida.

The vet tugged at the collar of his white lab coat. "Well, Bunny Whitaker gave me a stern talking-to about my relocation plan."

"I hope she told you that you could get fifty grand over the asking price for your house if you have me convert that butler's pantry into a home office."

"No, son. She made me admit how miserable I was living so far away from Birdie. So I took my house off the market and moved back here."

Bunny and Birdie Whitaker were the seventy-something-year-old sisters who owned Whitaker Acres and who had started the Furever Paws Animal Rescue years before. Though they'd never married or had children of their own, they'd become sort of surrogate aunts to most of the town, taking every-one under their wings—especially any animal in need. Bunny had turned up with a secret beau last year, and everyone knew about Doc J and Birdie getting together, only to have the relationship seem to end when the vet went to Florida.

But now it sounded like they were together again? Harris wished them well, either way, but wasn't interested in poking around into what had happened. Normally, he didn't listen to gossip unless it involved someone buying or selling real estate. And the Whitaker sisters happened to own some prime real estate that they'd probably never sell.

Doc J began examining the cat in Elise's arms, then had her move the animal to the stainless steel table. Oliver didn't like that one little bit, but his claws couldn't get any traction on the metal surface, leaving him slipping and sliding as he tried to get away. The door sprang open suddenly and Harris stood to prevent the frightened tabby from making another escape.

"Oliver?" A little blonde girl called as she pushed past Harris and ran into the crowded room. "Is it really you?"

The cat froze, then immediately began purring when Brooklyn Hobbs hugged Oliver to her chest. "Oh, Oliver, I missed you so much. I never stopped looking. I promise I'll never leave the back door open again. I love you and we're going to take you home and..." The rest of the child's words were lost as she buried her face in the matted orange fur.

Brooklyn's mom was standing just outside the door and Harris had to move behind Elise to make room for everyone inside the small exam area. "I can't believe you guys found him!" Renee Hobbs said, wiping a tear from her eye as she watched her daughter's emotional reunion with the missing pet.

"I thought for sure we'd never… I mean…after so long with no clues, it was hard to…"

Harris immediately understood what the mom was trying to say. "Well, he was certainly a clever little guy to be on his own for so long and he seems to have had quite an adventure."

"Thank you so much for finding him," Brooklyn told Harris.

"Well, technically, it wasn't me who found him. It was Miss Elise who recognized Oliver from your flyers." But the woman standing so close to him didn't say a word. In fact, she'd barely said anything since they'd arrived. Harris kept talking so she didn't have to. "That was so smart of you to post so many lost cat signs around town, Brooklyn."

"I colored it myself and then Mommy made copies with her scanner." The child beamed proudly up at him. "So where was he?"

Harris tried to replicate the same animated expression his own mom made whenever she'd recount some adventurous tale to her sons or her students. "Oliver was with a feral colony in that wooded area behind Maple Street."

"What does a *feral colony* mean?"

"It's like a group of cat friends that all hang out and eat together."

"Don't they have owners who feed them and love them?" The child's eyes were wide and worried. Based on her dedication and devotion to her own lost pet, he could only imagine how she'd take the news that there were more strays out there on the streets.

Harris looked to Doc J to help explain, but the vet had the stethoscope in his ears. Elise was biting on her lower lip, not likely to speak up either. Harris shrugged. "Most of them don't really have houses of their own. But they're happy to live outdoors and come and go when they please."

"Like those people who set up the carnival at my school over the summer?"

"Yeah. Kinda like that. Except instead of eating snow cones and cotton candy, they get to eat Feline Finest and canned tuna." Harris felt a sharp elbow jab his rib cage and he smothered a smile. "And they can't have bounce houses, of course, because their little claws would pop them like a balloon."

Brooklyn giggled, revealing a missing incisor.

"So he's definitely lost some weight," Doc J started, then stopped when he saw Brooklyn blink back another set of tears. "But he should easily be able to fatten up again with some good healthy food. I'm going to give him a topical cream for the—"

"So what was your favorite carnival ride, Brooklyn?" Harris asked, trying to distract the child from the conversation Doc J was having with Brooklyn's mom about the unhealed sore he'd noticed on Oliver's hind leg.

"The Ferris wheel because you can see everything from up there. But sometimes it feels like it takes forever to get all the way to the top."

"I agree. The view is great, but there's way too many stops on the way up. I like the bumper cars best."

"One time, I was doing the bumper cars and I crashed straight into Mrs. Patel. She's the principal at my school. Then Jonah Collins crashed into her next and all the other kids did too and she couldn't get away."

"A classic pileup." Harris nodded. "Nice."

"Yeah, it was super funny, but then she had to wear this weird bandage around her neck for a whole week."

"But she ended up being fine, right? Just like Oliver would be fine if he had to wear some kind of bandage for a little while."

Harris did his best to keep the child engaged as Doc J gave Oliver a shot of antibiotics and then put a cone of shame collar around his furry neck. As the four of them walked outside, both Brooklyn and her mom thanked Elise and Harris several more times before they finally left with a very sleepy and happy Oliver.

"You were amazing with her," Elise finally spoke after the girl and her mother had driven off.

"Thanks." Harris rubbed his sore ribs where Elise had jabbed him earlier over that tuna reference. "I've been told that I can be charming on occasion."

"I'm sure you *have* been told that." Her smile was so wide and her brown eyes were so bright, it nearly took Harris's breath away.

Her clothes weren't exactly eye-catching—except for this particular shirt with the missing button—and anytime he'd seen her out in public, she always stood in the background, so quiet and unobtrusive. It was like she purposely didn't want to be seen. But with her hair loosely held back like that, just a few brown waves framing her heart-shaped face, and with that beautiful, beaming smile…she was actually quite pretty. It was almost as though she suddenly had a light radiating from around her.

He cleared his throat again, a habit he'd never had around other women. "So I don't know about you, but I'm starved. What do you say we grab some dinner before I take you home?"

"Oh." Elise scanned the empty parking lot, as though she was hoping someone would come to her rescue. "We left so quickly, I…uh…didn't bring my purse."

"Well, if it's money you're worried about, I have my wallet."

"You can't keep offering to pay for things, Harris. I may be broke, but I have some pride." It was the first time she'd used his name, but he didn't get to enjoy it because her words made him feel as though he was breaking some unknown rule. "Besides, I think I left my purse sitting in my unlocked car back at the house. With a couple of bags of groceries that I forgot to put in the fridge."

"Fair enough. Then I'll drive you home." He held open the passenger door for her, half expecting her to bristle at that offer, as well. But she said nothing as she got in and quickly used the seat belt to hold her blouse closed again.

When he got in his truck, he told himself to give her a few minutes to relax and forget about their financial disparities. Then he'd change the subject and get Elise talking again.

But when he went to start the engine, all he heard was a brief sputter. He tried again, but it still wouldn't turn over. "That's weird. It never does this."

Elise bit her lower lip, making him worry that she was nervous at the thought of being stuck in this parking lot alone with him. Great.

"It's not the battery because the lights are working." He pushed several buttons and levers and then tried again. This time, nothing—not even a sputter. He swallowed a groan of frustration.

His parents were currently traveling with an RV adventure club they'd joined when they'd retired, so he hated to bother his dad. Instead, he picked up his phone to call his brother for mechanical advice when Elise quietly asked, "Do you mind if I take a look under the hood?"

Chapter Three

When Elise was fourteen and had no choice but to move in with her aunt, Regina had insisted they sell her dad's belongings—including his tool collection—to help pay for the pricey care center. Her aunt tried to make Elise feel better by telling her that men didn't like women who knew more about cars than they did anyway.

But Aunt Regina had probably never been stuck in a broken-down truck with her hot landlord who wanted to buy her dinner.

As if that was a bad thing. Elise shook her head as she got out of the vehicle. Most women would love to go out on a date with Harris Vega. The difference was that she knew it wouldn't be an actual date.

Once he got the hood open, it took Elise less than a minute to figure out the problem. "One of the wires to the spark plug is loose. If you have a torque wrench and some needle-nose pliers in your toolbox, I can tighten it."

"Wow. That's pretty embarrassing that I didn't know that." Harris dragged a hand through his dark hair, and Elise found herself wondering if he was one of those guys who paid top dollar at a high-end salon to achieve that casually disheveled look.

"It's okay. Lots of people wouldn't have caught it."

Uh-oh. Maybe her aunt had been right and Harris would resent her for making him seem incompetent at fixing his own truck.

Harris went to retrieve the tools, and when he handed them to Elise, he didn't look annoyed or really all that embarrassed. In fact, he smiled as he shrugged one shoulder. "I've never been very good with cars. Which is wild because my dad opened a mechanic shop that my brother still runs. They both tried to teach me, but I'd always end up getting distracted with the tools and using them to build something out of wood. I mean I understand the basics and can change a tire or jump-start a battery, but my skillset is geared more toward construction. I promise I'm pretty decent with my hands."

Elise ducked her head under the hood before he could see that she was blushing again at his last sentence. Harris seemed to have that effect on her, above and beyond her usual shyness. One of the groomers at Barkyard Boarding had said the same thing about his handiwork and it hadn't had any impact on Elise whatsoever.

Yet as she tightened the wire, all she could think about was how great it would feel to have Harris's hands on her.

She took a few steadying breaths before calling out, "Okay, try it again."

This time when he turned the ignition, the engine fired right up.

"Way to go, Lise!" Harris yelled over the running motor. "You are definitely full of surprises."

Pride was an unusual feeling for Elise, but there was definitely an extra jolt of satisfaction as she firmly closed the hood and wiped her hands on the back of her jeans. "My dad was kind of a car enthusiast."

"Yeah, I'm pretty sure everyone in North Carolina knows how much John Mackenzie loved cars. I still remember those commercials for Mackenzie Motors."

Elise's father had started off working for a used car lot right out of high school. He soon became one of their top salespeople and bought his own dealership. Then he bought several more. By the time

Elise was nine years old, Mackenzie Motors had expanded into several different states, with celebrities and professional athletes lining up to star in his famously quirky commercials. But then Elise's mom had gotten sick, and her dad sold off the business to have more time to care for his wife and daughter. Everything had gone downhill from there.

She gave her head a little shake, determined to focus on only the happy memories. "Yeah, well, most of my childhood was spent going to car shows and watching him tinker in his garage, refurbishing his classic cars."

"Apparently you weren't just watching him." Harris nodded at the wrench still in her hand.

Another unexpected burst of pride coursed through her. Elise might not have ever had a real job before Barkyard Boarding, but she'd overhauled engines and refurbished carburetors and even installed a complete brake system on a 1973 Chevy Nova when she was thirteen. Not that she needed to brag about it. It was something she'd shared with just her dad. He'd been proud of her, and that had been more than enough.

The emotional high didn't last long, though, and she was yawning by the time she climbed inside the truck again. It had been a long day and an even longer afternoon. She still reeked of tuna and feral cat, and the only thing she wanted to do at that second was go home and take a hot shower. And to forget about the way Harris Vega was always studying her with a mixture of surprise and curiosity.

"You probably don't remember this," Harris said when he pulled onto the highway to head back toward town. "But we met before, when we were kids."

Elise didn't remember any meeting—but it seemed plausible. Even though Elise had grown up in Raleigh, where Mackenzie Motors had been headquartered, they'd come to Spring Forest a lot. It was John Mackenzie's hometown and where he'd opened his first car dealership. His family had stayed local, and even after Elise's grandparents passed, they still came to town regularly to visit Uncle Tom and his new wife Regina, who'd loved hosting lavishly themed events. "Was it at one of my aunt's over-the-top parties?"

"Ha! Definitely not. My father was a mechanic who emigrated here from Mexico. My family wasn't exactly rubbing elbows with the upper-class socialites back then."

Even though Harris chuckled politely, Elise knew that his experience as a second-generation Mexican American in a blue-collar family would have been way different than her own privileged childhood. Her heart twisted with guilt. "I'm so sorry, Harris. That was such a thoughtless assumption to make."

His smile was warm and genuine. "It's okay.

I'm pretty sure I would've hated Regina's parties anyway."

"Well, I definitely couldn't stand them. Although, I don't really like *any* parties."

"Yeah, that's what I remember most about the first time we met. It was at the annual company picnic for Mackenzie Motors—where my dad worked. I was probably eleven or twelve. I think you might've been five or six."

"Eight," she said correcting him. "If you were eleven, then I was eight."

He stopped at an intersection and shifted in his seat to stare at her. "How do you know our exact age difference?"

She squeezed her eyes shut. Obviously, she couldn't admit that she'd been so curious, she'd googled him before moving into the Maple Street house. The top result was one of those "Top Thirty Under Thirty" articles spotlighting the successful and young entrepreneurs in North Carolina. Twenty-eight-year-old Harris had been on the list and while it was impressive, it was also a bit demoralizing that she was only three years younger and hadn't accomplished a single thing. "I think there was a magazine in my dentist's office that mentioned you?"

"Oh God. Not the one with me in the faded blue shirt? My mom was so mad that I wore something with a rip in it during a photo shoot. I told her I was working and I don't wear my church clothes to haul lumber. Anyway, if you were eight back then, then you were a tiny thing." Harris's eyes traveled down her torso and stopped at her legs. "You still are."

At this point, the embarrassing blush was never going to leave her cheeks. Luckily, the light changed to green and she could pretend to focus on the trees racing by way too quickly outside the passenger window. "So, our parents introduced us at the company picnic?"

"Not exactly. You sat off all alone with your mom. Didn't leave her side. My dad said I should go ask you if you wanted to play cornhole with me and some of the other kids. I told him you looked stuck-up."

She whipped her head in his direction. "I wasn't stuck-up!"

"No, I realize that now. You're just painfully shy."

"I don't try to be." She crossed her arms across her midsection. "It's just that I'm not very good interacting with people."

"You've interacted with me just fine all afternoon. But then we got to the shelter, and you just sort of clammed up."

"I didn't really see a need to say much since you were doing most of the talking." Not to mention, the last thing Elise wanted to do was have someone notice her and then ask about her aunt. "Like I said before, you were great with Brooklyn Hobbs back there. The way you distracted her when Doc J was talking to her mom about possible infections was perfectly timed. And then how you made it seem like Oliver had some grand adventure with his feral cat buddies? It reminded me of…"

There she went, trailing off again. But this time, Harris wasn't going to let her off the hook. "Who did I remind you of?"

She took a fortifying breath. "My dad. He had the same ability to put people at ease. It's probably why he could sell so many cars."

"I will definitely take that as a compliment. John Mackenzie was a good man. He left behind a pretty great legacy." He glanced across the truck at her long enough to give her a knowing smile.

Elise's chest felt lighter, hoping that Harris was referring to *her* being the legacy. Although maybe he was just talking about her father's legendary commercials that were forever documented on You-Tube. Because Lord knew there wasn't a single dime left from John Mackenzie's financial legacy.

"Elise? Is everything okay?" Harris asked when he answered his phone late the following Friday night. He'd been going through his materials list for the upcoming week and trying to figure out how he could be in multiple locations at once to accommodate all the deliveries. Even though Harris had a

strict company policy about his crews never working on the weekends, he rarely observed that rule
himself. But there was no way Elise would know
that, making it more likely that she'd only reach
out if it was an emergency.

"Oh, um, yeah. Everything is fine. Mostly. It's
just that I'm having a little trouble with the shower
in the master bathroom."

Harris shifted his laptop and paperwork to the
nightstand and sat up straighter in bed. He could tell
from the sound of her voice that she was trying to
downplay whatever the issue was. It was well estab-
lished by now that the woman didn't like drawing
any attention to herself. There was no way she'd
voluntarily cause an issue by complaining about
something minor.

"What kind of trouble?"

"Well, I was trying to change out the showerhead, and, um, let's just say that I'm the complete
opposite of you. *My* expertise with tools only ap-
plies to cars and not to plumbing. I think I made
the situation worse."

"Let me throw on some clothes and I'll be right
over," he said, then heard her gasp.

"No! You don't need to stop…uh…whatever
you're doing and…uh…get dressed." The last two
words came out in a high-pitched squeak. "It can
wait until morning."

What exactly did she think he was doing on a Friday night undressed?

Ohhh.

"No. I was just finishing some work in bed. Alone." He had to stifle a laugh. As much as he enjoyed the thought of her picturing him between the sheets, he didn't want to make her even more uncomfortable than she clearly already was. "It's really no trouble for me to come switch out the showerhead right now."

"Yeah, so that's the thing. It's not going to be a simple switch-out anymore. The broken one wasn't being too cooperative. There was a bit of a struggle and, well, I'm afraid I broke the exposed pipe. But the good news is that I finally found the shut-off valve for the water. So, it's no longer spraying everywhere."

Harris had to bite the inside of his cheek when she said there'd been a struggle. He would've liked to witness a petite but determined Elise wrestling with an uncooperative and outdated faucet system. Yet he also knew that it had probably taken just as much determination for her to admit defeat and call him for help. "I should probably come over tonight and check it out. Mrs. O'Malley never told me the shower didn't work."

"Judging by all the bottles of scented salt crystals and foaming bubbles she left behind, I'm guessing Mrs. O'Malley preferred baths anyway. Not that I blame her. I mean, the claw-foot tub is practically a work of art. And it's pretty relaxing after a long day at work. But it wasn't super practical for washing my hair, which is why I tried to fix the shower myself."

The sudden—and rather enjoyable—image of Elise Mackenzie bathing was just as quickly replaced with one of flooded hardwood floors and soaking wet drywall caused by a major leak. "Still, I should've done a walk-through before you moved in to check for issues like that. I promise I'm not one of those landlords who never fixes anything to save a buck." He accidentally let out a yawn. "Apparently, I *am* one of those landlords who overcommits to too many properties and doesn't always have time to keep up on the repairs."

"Harris, my rent is half of what it should be specifically so I can make those little fixes around the place. I never expected everything to start out in perfect shape. Besides, you added me to your account at the hardware store—which was how I bought the new showerhead in the first place, by the way. Nobody would ever accuse you of being a cheap landlord. And I promise the repairs can wait until tomorrow. The only reason I bothered you so late was because I wanted you to hear about the broken pipe directly from me and not from Reverend Johnson next door. I'm afraid I woke up him and a couple other neighbors with some unfortunate language choices when I was stumbling around the side yard in the dark searching for the valve to shut off the water."

His eyes widened in curiosity, but his guilt kept him from asking her to repeat the words she used. "I should've at least walked the property with you and showed you where it was."

"Roxy Cole, the teenager from across the street, heard the commotion, and came over with her dachshund and a flashlight to help me find the valve. But then Mr. Frankfurter saw a raccoon run by and he slipped his leash, chasing the poor thing right through the fence of the Winchells' prized vegetable garden. The reverend went home complaining that he'll never get enough sleep before the three wedding ceremonies he's performing tomorrow. The Winchells' two-pound zucchini is now only half that size and won't take home any prizes at the Spring Forest Squash Festival next month. Oh, and Mr. Frankfurter has to go get a rabies shot because he wasn't expecting the raccoon to actually fight back. But everyone is okay for now."

Elise sighed when she finally concluded her long-winded account of everything that had gone wrong. She sounded as exhausted as he felt. Harris barely managed to hold back his laughter as he looked at the late hour on his bedside clock.

"Fine. If you're positive things are okay for now, then I'll wait and come over first thing in the morning to fix it. And for what it's worth, I'm really sorry that you had to go through all of this tonight." Although, hearing her tell the story had been fairly entertaining.

"Don't be. At least not on my behalf. I've now met everyone who lives on this block of Maple Street. That's a first for me."

He could have sworn he heard a hint of pride in her voice and found himself smiling as he fell asleep.

Harris was still chuckling to himself on his drive over to Maple Street the next morning. He couldn't stop thinking about the very quiet and very reserved Elise Mackenzie blurting out a stream of frustrated curse words loud enough to wake the entire neighborhood. Or at least set off a chain of events to wake the neighborhood.

Every time he turned around, he learned something new about the young woman, something unexpected. When he knocked on Elise's door a few minutes later, he was even more surprised to find that she'd made him breakfast. "Come in and eat first."

"Well, I'm not going to say no to a home-cooked breakfast." He sat down at the small kitchen table, which held plates of warm fluffy pancakes, bacon straight out of a cast iron skillet, cheesy scrambled eggs, and even a hot pot of coffee. "How did you do all of this with no running water?"

Elise jerked her thumb toward the hallway leading to the mudroom. There were at least ten jugs of water lined up. "Several of the neighbors brought those over last night after everything calmed down. Oh, and Reverend Johnson said I could use his bathroom until mine got fixed, as long as I promised not to take the Lord's name in vain anymore."

"They think it's going to take me that long to fix it? How badly broken is the pipe?" He shoved a forkful of syrup-drenched pancakes into his mouth, then closed his eyes in bliss. "Wow. This is incredible. I can't remember the last time someone cooked me a meal. I mean, someone who wasn't related to me or didn't work in a restaurant."

"Maybe I'm hoping to convince you that I'm not an annoying tenant who should be paying more rent."

"I think *I'm* the one getting the bargain. Did you know that I haven't had pancakes in at least three months? Ever since my parents retired and moved to Ashville, my mom worries that I don't eat enough. But if the restaurants I went to served food this good, that wouldn't be a problem."

Elise held her coffee mug to her lips but couldn't disguise the fact that her eyes were traveling down the length of Harris's torso. His biceps flexed involuntarily, as though to prove he was in pretty good shape.

She must've swallowed too much coffee because she made a little choking sound. "So do you eat *all* of your meals out?"

"Mostly. It depends on whether I have a working kitchen at any given time."

She tilted her head. "You remodel your own kitchen that often?"

"No, I mean I don't exactly have a permanent home. I usually just live in whichever house I'm working on. It makes for an easy commute."

"How many houses do you own? Besides this one, I mean."

"Currently, I own nine. I think."

"You *think*?"

He did a quick inventory in his head. "Plus a couple of commercial properties downtown. But after I fix a place up, I usually turn around and sell it. I have a spreadsheet on my laptop, but I'm always in the middle of buying or selling something, so the number changes a lot."

"Doesn't that get confusing? Not really having a central location?"

"Oh, I have an office. It's at the old Henderson farm out on Little Creek Road. I parceled off some of the land to the city for that primary connector to Spring Forest Boulevard, then retrofitted the barn into a shop of sorts to store all my equipment and surplus building supplies. I turned the upstairs loft into an apartment and was living there for awhile. But a few years ago, Buster, my job foreman, needed a place to stay so I insisted he move in there."

Elise scratched her head, knocking her loose ponytail askew. "So let me get this straight. You could be living in a custom-built apartment. Or even here at this house or in one of the other ones you own. But instead you bounce around from construction zone to construction zone because…why?"

"Because other people need those places more." His stomach was full, but everything tasted so good that he kept reaching for more in spite of himself until he had to force himself to scoot his chair away from the table.

Yet Elise didn't appear to be in any hurry to move away from this conversation. In fact, she now had her chin propped in both of her hands as she studied him. Was this what he looked like when he was watching her just as closely, trying to figure out what made her tick? No wonder she avoided making eye contact with him so much.

Harris, who never sat still long enough for anyone to give him a second glance, let alone scrutinize him so intensely, stood. "How about we go check out that broken pipe?"

Chapter Four

"Didn't the shower in here used to be enclosed?" Harris asked after he finished soldering a new piece of copper pipe. "I could've sworn it had one of those funky seventies-era frosted glass doors."

Elise hadn't meant to sit in the bathroom with him while he worked. There were plenty of things she could've been doing around the house and yard. But he'd kept asking her to pass him tools and then he started asking her opinion on tile styles. Before too long, it was just easier to stay in here rather than keep coming back in from the kitchen every time he called out to her.

"I think so. I found the door leaning against the shed in the backyard. There was a huge crack in it."

Harris's lips formed an O as he sucked in a hiss. "I really hope Mrs. O'Malley didn't haul it out there herself. One little slip and there would've been shattered glass everywhere."

Elise shouldn't have been surprised at his concern for the former owner. The man was proving himself to be quite the generous landlord. She'd fully expected him to be angry about her breaking the pipe last night. Yet he'd been the one to apologize to *her*. Then, after talking to several of the neighbors she'd met last night, Elise had found out that when he'd bought the Craftsman-style bungalow from Mrs. O'Malley, he could've easily flipped it and made a sweet profit right away. Instead, he'd rented it to her for way under market value, even with her tackling some of the cleanup renovations herself.

"Judging by the rusty nails it was leaning against, I think the crack happened after she hauled it out of here."

"Why would she get rid of a perfectly good—albeit ugly—glass door just because the showerhead wasn't working?"

"Probably because she was using this area for storage. I found an old sewing machine back here, several bolts of fabric, and about ten years' worth of quilting magazines. Oh, and a case of glitter spray paint that I'm currently trying to figure out a use for."

"So she kept all her crafting supplies in the bathroom?" He pointed to the new showerhead Elise had chosen. "Will you pass me that?"

"Storing the stuff here makes more sense than where she kept her cat figurine collection." She opened the plastic packaging before handing him the plain, no-frills nozzle. "My dad was like that, too, when he first got diagnosed with Alzheimer's. Putting things in random places and never getting rid of anything. It makes sense to them, which is all that matters."

Harris paused, his wrench midturn, and looked in her direction. Elise wished she hadn't brought up her father again. It was always uncomfortable when people didn't know what to say or how to react.

She wiped her already clean hands on her jeans and pretended to focus on the sink area. "The hardware store had an amazing collection of retro brass-plated fixtures that would've looked amazing in here with those gold-toned drawer pulls. But then I saw the price for the coordinating showerhead and faucet handles and went for function over style. Besides, since I'm using some of the leftover fabric I found to make a shower curtain, it's not like anyone will see the hardware in there anyway."

"*You'll* see it," Harris said.

"Well, yeah. But it's not like I'm going to have

guests or anything." Great. Now Elise sounded like a total loser with no friends. Although, that wasn't exactly far from the truth.

"For the record, I don't mind spending a little extra money if it's going to help the resale value of the house later on." Harris must've seen her startled expression because he held up his palm as though he could stop her thoughts. "Not that I'm planning on selling this place anytime soon."

That was a relief because Elise didn't know of any other places she could afford. There was a long-term residence hotel in town that was cheap—but it was also pretty sketchy. That would be an absolute last resort.

"That ought to do it," he said as he gave one last turn of his wrench. "I'm going to go switch the water on so you can test the plumbing before I put my tools away."

Elise didn't think she'd ever be the type of woman who would get emotional about something so simple as a working shower, but a couple of minutes later when the spray came out in a steady stream she whooped with excitement.

"I take it that we were successful," Harris said as he returned to the bathroom.

"Not *we*," Elise corrected him. "You."

"Yeah, but only because you power-loaded me with the best coffee and pancakes in all of North Carolina."

"I'm sure they weren't the best. Especially since I'm out of practice. When I moved in with my aunt, she insisted on a low-carb diet and didn't allow any food she thought would be fattening."

Harris narrowed his eyes. "She thought you needed to lose weight?"

"No. But if Regina was dieting, everyone around her was dieting because she didn't like having temptation present in the house at all. She was really big on appearances and was always trying to get me to dress up or make more of an effort. I learned pretty quickly, though, that the best way to keep her from dragging me to so many events was to stay as plain as I possibly could. If I didn't look the part of a socialite, she wouldn't force me to be one."

"For what it's worth," Harris said as his gaze leisurely traveled over her body, which was difficult to do since they were in such a tight space. "I think you look great just the way you are."

As soon as the first flicker of heat traveled from her neck to her face, Elise quickly bolted out of the tiny bathroom before she made a fool of herself.

Again.

Crap. Harris hadn't intended to scare the woman away or sound as though he was putting the moves on her. He just thought Elise deserved to hear the truth. Plus, finding out she had a bit of a rebellious streak when it came to her aunt made her that much more attractive.

Okay so Elise Mackenzie was attractive. It wasn't a crime to notice that fact as long as neither one of them got the wrong impression about each other.

Once, earlier in his career, he'd been so enthusiastic about a new house he was buying, the single—and rather flirtatious—real estate agent mistakenly thought all his eager requests for after-hours walkthroughs and inspections were intended as romantic advances. When Harris told her to bring protective wear to christen the new place after the escrow signing, he'd meant a hard hat and a sledgehammer. Not the industrial-sized box of condoms and bottle of champagne the agent was holding when she opened the door and found him standing there with his entire demo crew.

Everyone except his unflappable job foreman had been understandably embarrassed that day, and Harris had sworn that he'd get better at reading people and communicating his business intentions—especially when there was an attractive woman involved.

The problem was that Elise clearly wasn't trying to flirt with him. So then why couldn't Harris stop wishing that she would?

"Stop it, man," he mumbled as he put his tools

away. "She's your tenant. Don't make things weird."

After convincing himself that he could keep things professional between them, he made his way back to the kitchen, determined not to bring up Elise's appearance again. "So, now that we've got a functioning shower, what's your next project?"

And that's when the woman really lit up.

Harris tried to focus on Elise's words and not on her lively face as she talked about her plans to rent a sander to refinish the floors. She pulled out a spiral notebook and all he could do was smile and nod eagerly as she jumped from one subject to another, going down a list of ideas she'd apparently been dying to share with someone. It was impossible for him not to feed off her same energy. Her hands were in constant movement and she barely paused for breaths as she explained several design ideas and the research she'd done.

"Obviously, some of the furniture is beyond saving." Elise was now pacing in the crowded living room. Harris realized he had no idea when they'd even left the kitchen. Yet he must have already followed her through the master bedroom and the dining room because his brain was full of mental notes about so many of her suggestions. "But, I've been watching some do-it-yourself videos online and I'm pretty sure that I can reupholster these two armchairs. And the dining room table seems to be in decent condition, but I have no idea where the chairs are for it. I'm thinking about driving to a consignment store in Raleigh after I get a few more paychecks to see what I can find there."

"I probably should have mentioned this before, but back at the shop I have some staging furniture we use when we have open houses. You should stop by and see if there's anything you could use."

"Are you serious?" Elise's eyes had gone even wider and brighter, like a kid who had just been invited to a shopping spree at a candy store. "I mean, I know it would only be temporary and you're not giving me anything, but I will make you a years' supply of pancakes if you can loan me a sofa that doesn't look like a family of squirrels have taken up residence in the cushions."

"That's a fair trade." His chest swelled with the satisfaction of being the one who brought her that much joy. "Can you bring the first batch tomorrow?"

When Elise pulled up to his shop the following morning in her old nondescript minivan that had seen better days, Harris found himself wondering how the only daughter of one of the most successful—and possibly wealthiest—car dealers in the state had ended up in such clearly dire financial straits. There had to be a story there. Or at least a simple enough explanation, like bad investments or compulsive spending habits—either of which seemed equally, sadly, likely, given that John had suffered from dementia. As much as he wanted to blurt out the question, he'd learned not to bring up her family unless she mentioned them first.

Being around Elise was a lesson in patience. He wasn't sure what the long-term result would be, but if he was rewarded with more smiles—and hopefully more food—then he was sure it would be worth it.

She opened the back hatch, revealing several aluminum pans, and Harris's mouth began to water before he made it across the driveway. "I didn't realize the year's supply of pancakes would be delivered all at once."

She beamed at him so brightly, he almost stumbled on the uneven gravel. It was becoming more difficult to slow this growing attraction to her when she looked at him like that.

"It's not just pancakes. I tried my hand at meal prepping for the week in advance so that I have more time to work on the house after my shifts. Unfortunately, I'm not used to cooking so much food at once and I overestimated. But hey, at least now I know I won't be a total bust if Josie Whitaker still wants me to help her out at the catering company."

He surveyed all the foil-covered containers. "I'm worried that I might've made my staging furniture collection seem a little bigger and better than it is."

"You're talking to a woman who is currently living in a house where all the window coverings are made from fabric printed with dancing cats."

Harris grinned as he picked up a stack of individually packaged meals. "Let's get these into the break room refrigerator, and then you can start finding some framed artwork to go with those beautiful cat curtains."

Twenty minutes later, Elise was making lists on a pad of paper and using a stack of Post-it notes to mark which items she wanted. She'd studied every single piece he owned, moving accent tables next to upholstered headboards and then bookshelves next to sofas. She'd even found a collection of lamps and throw pillows that he hadn't known he had.

"Are you sure you don't mind me taking this dresser too? I was hoping I could throw a coat of paint on the one in the extra bedroom, but when I pulled it away from the wall the other day to clean behind there, the back of it was covered with this weird fuzzy white mold."

"Okay. That's gross. But it also reminds me that I scheduled a dumpster to be delivered to your house on Tuesday. I knew Mrs. O'Malley had been a hoarder, but I hadn't realized how much stuff she'd left behind. I'll also have Buster and a few of the guys come by one day this week to help you fill it."

She turned from the metal rack holding several

rolled-up area rugs. "I thought you said you were understaffed right now?"

"I am. But I just got a call that my custom cabinet delivery is running late, and the crew can't begin the next phase until it arrives. I could have them start reroofing the Victorian on Second Street, but once you pull the old shingles and paper off, you have to stay and finish getting the new ones on before it rains. It's all or nothing with roofing, and if we do everything now, it'll end up causing an even bigger delay for the kitchen project. Then the electrician gets backed up and the whole thing becomes a scheduling nightmare."

"Wow. Now I know why my aunt had such a hard time finding a local handyman. She was always hiring new people she found online who rarely stayed long enough to finish the job."

Probably because no contractor in Spring Forest wanted to work for Elise's aunt. When Harris had first started his business, one of his flooring suppliers warned him that Regina Mackenzie was impossible to please and always found a reason not to pay the final installment of her contract.

Instead of saying as much, he turned to the giant dry-erase board on the wall outside of his office. The grids of the calendar were completely full. "I keep trying to tell myself that things will calm down a little after Halloween. One of my guys returns from family leave by then, and Buster's cousin is hoping to start as soon as he finalizes his military discharge paperwork. So reinforcements are on the way, but what I really need is a designer."

Elise stopped unrolling the rug she'd maneuvered to the ground between them. She was in a squatting position and had to crane her neck to look up at him. "You have a designer?"

"I hired one a few years ago. In fact, she's the one who organized all of this." He gestured to the area of the shop where all the staging furniture was so well itemized. Hence the reason why he hadn't realized he'd acquired so much over the years—that had never been his department. "When I first remodeled the barn, I hired her to create a showroom type of area where I could have clients come see examples of my work. But then I started taking on fewer jobs for hire and started flipping the houses I already owned. Adina stayed on part-time and was a genius at getting the houses ready to sell. Sometimes we'd get well over asking price if we agreed to leave the home furnished as is."

"Wow. That job sounds pretty amazing. Why'd she leave?"

"Because she got an offer from one of those home improvement shows on TV." Harris didn't mention that he'd also been offered a spot on the same show. But he had no desire to be on television or to leave Spring Forest. "I was really excited for her at the time, but now I'm struggling finding someone to fill her shoes. Which was why I was hoping that you—" He stopped midsentence when he realized Elise was adamantly shaking her head. "Why are you already saying no? I haven't even asked yet."

"Harris, I'm not a designer. I barely know a herringbone inlay from a Chantilly parquet."

He pointed at her. "But you *do* know the difference. I need someone who gets excited about taking on a new project and has your vision. All the ideas you showed me back at your house? I can tell they sound great—but they're definitely more than I ever could have come up with myself. Ever since Adina left, I've been playing it safe with the same neutral tones and subway tiles. The other day Buster told me all our houses are becoming too cookie-cutter."

Elise opened and closed her mouth several times. Finally she said, "But I already have a job at Barkyard Boarding. I like working with the animals."

"This would only be part-time. In fact, less than part-time. You could make your own hours and stop by the jobsites whenever you have a chance. You mentioned working for Josie's catering company to earn some extra money. Why don't you work for me instead?"

"Don't you think that would be awkward if we… uh…worked together?"

"How so?"

She squeezed her eyes shut. "Because you already let me live at the Maple Street house way too cheaply. If you give me a sympathy job, people are going to think it's…you know…suspicious."

"No, it's just good business sense. Vega Homes is booming, and I really could use the help." He stopped short of mentioning the symmetry of her dad seeing potential in his dad and giving him a chance all those years ago—and now him doing the same for her. He liked the idea of paying it forward, but he worried that mentioning the connection between their fathers might cause Elise to think he was only offering her extra work out of some old family debt. "You needed a place to rent, I needed someone who could help me fix up one of my rental properties. I need a designer, you need a part-time job. I'll even throw in a full set of kitchen cabinets for the house you're in now. Custom ones."

Elise clutched her hand to her heart. That's when he knew he'd made the right decision to offer her the job. "In pale blue? Like the ones in that magazine shoot you did for the Top Thirty Under Thirty article? And a new countertop?"

"I happen to have a case of quartz and granite samples in my truck. You can pick them out right now."

"I don't have any experience as a designer, though. I mean, I used to help my aunt with ideas and layouts any time she got bored and wanted to remodel a room in her house. But I'm certainly not qualified to replace someone who landed a job on a TV show."

Harris pointed to a little wooden sign hanging above the exit door. It was the last thing he saw every time he left the building. It was lovingly stenciled by hand with the words *Take A Chance*.

"See that? My parents and my brother have matching signs. I guess you could say it's the Vega family motto. See, my dad moved to a brand-new country when he was barely out of high school. A few years later, he met my mom on a blind date intended for her roommate, who was too nervous to go herself. My mom volunteered to go as a stand-in—or as she called herself, *an understudy*—and my folks ended up falling in love. Did I mention my mom always had us auditioning for stuff growing up? Everyone, especially me, knew I wouldn't get a part, but I still gave it a shot. And you know what? All those auditions helped me with my presentation skills, which came in handy when I was twenty years old, with no credit and needed to convince an investor to help me buy my first house to flip. So how about it? What do you say to taking a chance?"

"What if I'm not any good?" She bit her lower lip, a move he now recognized as something she did whenever she seemed uncertain. It was also something she did that he couldn't take his eyes off of.

He shook his head to clear the seductive image,

not wanting to lose this opportunity. He was a businessman who always sealed the deal.

"Lise, you'll never know unless you try."

Chapter Five

Elise had always been uncomfortable with the unhealthy power imbalance between her and Regina. Not that her reluctant guardian was abusive or even mean, really. In fact, her aunt could be very generous. Her fundraisers had been a godsend to plenty of charities over the years. And she was the one who'd stepped up to pay for Elise's father's care after all the money was gone. Elise would never forget that. But… Aunt Regina would never let *her* forget it either. The weight of what Elise owed always hung in the air. When Elise moved out of her aunt's house, she promised to never let herself feel indebted to anyone like that again. Especially now that she was finally gaining the confidence of being on her own.

Then along came Harris Vega who insisted that giving Elise a deal on the rent and hiring her part-time was purely a business arrangement. He'd made it sound as though Elise would be the one doing *him* a favor. While her confidence had slowly improved with every scrap of independence she earned, there was no way she could convince herself that the man truly *needed* her help. Especially after finding out how he'd given similar rental deals to his foreman and probably anyone else who came along. Elise was likely just another one of his charity cases.

Still.

She needed the extra money. Besides, she'd already succumbed to the idea the second she'd walked in the door and seen all the surplus staging furniture. Everything about the huge remodeled barn felt right. Just like being with the animals at Barkyard Boarding had felt right.

"Fine," she told Harris, who pumped a fist in the air. Before he could get too excited, she cautioned, "I'll help you with some design ideas, but *only* until you find someone more qualified."

"I'll take whatever I can get." His smile was nearly contagious. "You are really saving my butt, Lise."

Later that afternoon, she pushed away her way-ward thoughts about his butt, as well as her increasing self-doubt, by clearing almost everything she could carry out of the living room and then sketching some ideas for her new kitchen cabinets. The only thing she'd allow herself to focus on was how positive things were starting to look for her, both inside her new home and out.

Yet when she arrived at Barkyard Boarding on Monday for her shift, Elise saw the schedule for the upcoming week and began to panic. The summer vacation rush was over, so they'd have fewer animals overnight. However, now that kids were back in school, the doggie day care program suddenly had a wait list and there was talk about adding an extra morning session.

What if Elise couldn't do it all? What if she was exactly like her aunt who overcommitted and then left necessary work unfinished? Her heart began to race from the extra cup of coffee this morning and her stomach felt as though she'd eaten way too many leftover pancakes before work.

She sucked in several slow, deep breaths, and just when she thought her anxiety was under control, Josie Whitaker walked in with her black-and-white cockapoo.

"Good morning." Elise hoped the squeaky pitch of her voice sounded more cheerful than startled. Josie had been the caterer for Aunt Regina's last luncheon soiree and suddenly, Elise wondered if her aunt had paid the final invoice before skipping town.

"Hey, Elise." Josie, with her great shape and messy blond ponytail, was proof that for some women the forties were the new twenties. "I'm dropping off Harlow for her grooming appointment."

Oh, thank God she wasn't here to collect on a debt. Elise would've sagged against the reception counter in relief if she wasn't already so jumpy from too much caffeine. "The groomer isn't here yet, but Harlow can hang out in the indoor play area while she waits."

"I hope you don't mind me bringing her a little early, but I've got two separate menu tastings today."

Now would've been the perfect opportunity to let Josie know that she couldn't help with any catering jobs since she was going to be busy helping Harris. But Elise wasn't sure how to say it without sounding ungrateful, or like she was taking a better offer. Her pulse began thrumming as she racked her brain for the best response. All she came up with was, "Wow. Sounds like you're getting lots of bookings."

"Actually, it's for the same booking. Apparently, the mother of the bride can't stand to be in the same room as the mother of the groom. Yet both women insist on approving every detail of the wedding.

Thank goodness I'm just the caterer and not the wedding planner."

The front door opened and Elise's racing heart nearly stopped in its tracks when Bethany Robeson walked inside the building. She had somehow managed to avoid the director of Furever Paws the past few weeks, yet she knew that sooner or later she'd have to face the woman. Especially since Bethany was engaged to Shane Dupree, Elise's boss.

Harlow let out a bark in recognition, probably since she and her littermates had been guests at the animal shelter after being rescued from a terrible backyard breeder situation. Bethany had been part of the team that had gotten the mistreated animals healthy and rehabilitated so that they could be adopted.

"Oh, look at how big you're getting," Bethany said to the pup. She set a cardboard tray of coffee drinks on the counter before bending down to scratch the mop of curls between the dog's ears.

Bethany gasped and pointed to Josie's left hand, which was holding the leash. "Is that what I think it is?"

Josie's smile was as bright as the diamond ring on her finger. "It is. Declan proposed as soon as the ink was dry on Harlow's adoption papers. I think his niece, Shannon, and my daughter, Hannah, picked out bridesmaid dresses before the weekend was over, practically. How are things going over at Furever Paws? Are my aunts still arguing over where to park Stew's RV?"

For a moment, Elise wracked her brain to remember who Stew was…oh, right. Bunny Whitaker's boyfriend.

Uh-oh. How could Elise forget? Josie was the niece of the Whitaker sisters. Spring Forest wasn't exactly a small town, but everyone in the animal community tended to know each other. Which meant they all probably knew about Regina missing in action, flaking out on her commitment.

"That was last week's drama," Bethany chuckled. "This week, we get to deal with the battle over the ancient coffee maker in the break room. Bunny and Birdie don't want to throw in the towel yet and buy a new one, but they're also the only ones who know how to work the temperamental thing. Shane found out I've been stopping by Whole Bean every morning and he made a comment about needing a double espresso to get through today's schedule. So I figured I'd surprise him. I brought an extra one for you, Elise."

The last thing Elise needed was any more caffeine. But she was also touched that Bethany had thought of her. She wasn't accustomed to people doing nice things for her, and there had been so many lately! First, Shane gave her the job at Barkyard Boarding, despite her complete lack of professional experience. Then Harris offered her the rental house, with no security deposit at a reduced rent. And now this. Maybe they weren't holding her responsible for her aunt's little disappearing act, after all. But by standing there and not saying anything, Elise felt the same sort of powerlessness she'd experienced when she'd been just another one of Regina's charity cases.

As much as she didn't want to bring up the elephant in the room, Elise couldn't pretend everything was okay. Staying silent would only make her more complicit. Or more of a victim. She didn't want to be either.

Elise steeled her spine and, before she lost her courage, blurted out, "I have no idea where my aunt is. Or why she left."

Both Josie and Bethany were wide-eyed and silent, probably shocked by Elise's sudden outburst about a subject they'd been too polite to mention. Great. Now she sounded like a madwoman *and* a charity case.

Yet this weight she hadn't realized she'd been carrying was much lighter, making her shoulders straighter with every word she spoke. "I had no clue that she was going to take off like this. I really hope that she didn't leave everyone in the lurch. But maybe it's a good thing that she's not around to interfere and we can just keep on planning the fashion show without her."

Josie and Bethany shared a look and Elise's

stomach sank. *Relax*, she told herself. *You just blurted out some unexpected information at once and maybe they're both just as stunned as Harris had been to hear you say more than a couple of sentences at a time.*

But unlike Harris, the two women weren't smiling at her. In fact, their expressions were rather pained. It was the same way the nurses at Horizons would look at her whenever she would visit her father. Everyone seemed to know how bad things were, but they wouldn't tell her, and once again she was a helpless little girl, on the outside looking in. Fighting the urge to run to the bathroom and lock herself in one of the privacy stalls, Elise asked, "What aren't you telling me?"

"The thing is…" Bethany clasped her hands in front of her. "We're not going to be able to hold the fundraiser this year. Most of the money to pay for the event is gone."

How could that be? Getting donations to pay for the events was the one part of hosting fundraisers that Aunt Regina had been really good at. "But I thought there was plenty of… Oh no." Elise remembered seeing a copy of the financial report and the donation checks when she'd taken her aunt's Mercedes to the car wash the day before the woman had left town. Realization hit her all at once. "Did…" She didn't even want to think it, let alone say it aloud. But as gut-churning as it was, she needed to know—especially since she was sure everyone else in town already knew. Being independent meant living in the real world and no longer hiding herself from the truth. She shook her head, but not in disbelief. In frustration. "My aunt took it all."

It wasn't a question. Or even an accusation. It was a fact. One Elise should've been aware of before now.

Josie looked back and forth between Bethany and Elise before saying, "How about I take Harlow back to the puppy play area to wait for the groomer so that you guys can talk?"

"Only if you want to." Elise didn't feel the need for privacy for herself, but she didn't want Josie to feel uncomfortable listening to such a personal and embarrassing conversation. Yet most people in town probably already knew and were talking about her aunt. Josie was the Whitakers' niece. It was only right that she stay and listen. "But I wouldn't mind you staying."

Finally, Bethany nodded. "It's fine for you to stay, Josie. And, Elise...you're right. It does look like Regina took the money when she left. We weren't necessarily worried at first. Regina was out of town, but she goes out of town a lot. Then she wasn't returning our calls, but Bunny and Birdie said she can be flighty—their words, not mine."

Elise held up a palm, stopping the woman from apologizing for saying something that was common enough knowledge. "They're not wrong. She isn't the most reliable person and has always taken off on a whim. But not for this long. And I can't imagine why she would have taken the donations. She never talked to me about money issues, unless it was to remind me how much she paid for my father's care."

"If it makes you feel any better," Bethany offered, "we didn't notice the money missing the first two weeks."

"But I *lived* with her. I should've seen this coming."

"Don't blame yourself," Josie insisted, but Elise wasn't convinced.

"Josie's right." Bethany nodded. "Even Bunny and Birdie gave her the benefit of the doubt and wanted to wait before getting the police involved. But we can't hold it off any longer. We're going to have to press charges."

Elise rocked on her heels, then wiped her palms on her jeans. "I already filed a missing persons report, but it was more of a formality since she'd clearly left of her own accord. I'd be happy to talk to the detectives, though, and help with their investigation. I saw the donation checks in her car the day before she left. I remember thinking that I needed to add them to the list of donors I kept on my laptop. Oh my gosh. My laptop. I have notes and spreadsheets and vendor contacts on there that I should send you."

Bethany reached out and patted her shoulder. "Maybe we can save those for next year's fundraiser. I just don't see it happening this year with our limited budget."

"Okay, I know you have no reason to trust me, given my family history. But…" Elise drew in a deep breath, steadying her nerves for the crazy idea she was about to throw out there. "I really think we could still pull it off. I know the first round of donations are gone, but we could still get some corporate sponsors. There's plenty of local businesses who might be willing to donate services or products for a silent auction."

Elise sounded ridiculous even to her own ears. While she was the one who had always handled the paperwork and the details of sponsorships, she'd never gone out door-to-door herself. She certainly wasn't the salesman her father was. But at least Bethany's head was slightly tilted in curiosity. Like she might actually be considering it.

"I don't know what you're thinking in terms of food." Josie unwound the leash that had become twisted around her legs as a restless Harlow did circles around her feet. "But if we do some simple appetizer stations instead of a full, multicourse meal, my catering company could cover the costs. It'd be good advertising for us."

Elise wanted to hug the woman for both her generous offer and for her vote of confidence. Instead, she quickly continued while she still had a somewhat captive audience.

"Also, I was thinking we could hold a virtual cutest pet contest to raise money. One thing I've learned working at Barkyard Boarding is that people who dote on their pets usually want others to love their precious fur babies as much as they do. Our clients are always willing to pay extra for added walks and one-on-one playtime. I've only been here a few weeks and already, I've practically become a professional photographer with how many picture requests I get from pet parents while they're at work or on vacation."

Bethany tapped her chin. "Like a beauty pageant?"

"Sort of." Elise nodded with excitement at the possibility. "I'm sure plenty of people would be willing to pay a small entrance fee to be able to post pictures of their animals online and have others vote for their favorites. The winner could get some sort of prize, like a supply of dog treats or a gift card for grooming services."

Harlow barked and gave a little tail wag, as though to give her approval. Josie knelt down to confer with her cockapoo. "What do you think, girl? I bet you could win a cutest pet contest. Especially after you get your hair done today."

Bethany laughed. "Looks like we've already got our first contestant."

Elise clasped her hands in front of her, barely able to keep herself from doing a celebratory spin. "I'll start working on a website—" She paused, realizing she might be coming across as overbearing as her aunt. "That is, if you want me to help out. If you want some time to think about it, and maybe consider someone else, that's okay too. I know the fundraiser is a big project and having me there might be an even bigger risk given everything that's going on with my aunt. But I assure you that you guys would still be in charge and I could just be behind the scenes throwing out ideas and running errands or even doing the manual labor. Whatever role you want me to have in this, I genuinely want to help raise money for the animals."

Bethany glanced at the calendar on the wall. "Well, if we're going to pull this off before Halloween still, we're going to need all the help we can get."

This time Elise did do a little celebratory bounce as relief washed through her. She was going to get a chance to make things right. She wasn't going to blow it.

"Come and meet the rest of the crew," Harris said early Friday morning when Elise parked on the street in front of the old colonial he'd just purchased.

His grin probably made him appear a bit too eager, but he just felt so relieved that she'd actually shown up. All week long, he'd half expected getting a phone call from her with some sort of excuse for why she couldn't work for him. In fact, he'd purposely avoided going to her house on Tuesday when the dumpster got delivered or on Wednesday when his guys were there filling it. He hadn't wanted to give her the opportunity to cancel.

Elise's eyes were wide—either with fascination or apprehension—as she watched the bulldozer beep in reverse away from what used to be the front porch with a full bucket of rotted boards and broken bits of concrete. He could barely hear her quiet voice above the shouts and banging and engine noise, but he was pretty sure she said, "I think I met everyone earlier this week."

Of course she had. Harris would've known that if he hadn't been too chicken to go over there himself. No, not chicken, he corrected himself. Cautious. He hadn't wanted to scare her off.

The bulldozer dumped its load into the huge metal bin, causing a loud crash and a cloud of mildew-scented dust. But Elise didn't flinch as she reached into her back seat and extracted a folder and a large brown paper bag.

"*Now* it's a good morning." Buster, the lead foreman, walked toward them with a sledgehammer slung over his beefy shoulder. "Please tell me you got some more of those chocolate chip cookies in there, Miss Mack."

"Actually, I was toying with a new oatmeal toffee chip recipe and brought those instead." Elise bypassed Harris as though he wasn't even there, then made her way into the yard, easily navigating some upended wicker furniture that had been dumped there rather hastily. "Don't worry, Buster. I didn't put any cinnamon in yours because of your allergy. And I only added pecans to Miguel's dozen since Tony and Owen said they hated nuts."

Harris felt something tugging the corners of his mouth into a frown as he jumped over a mold-covered porch swing cushion. It wasn't that he was jealous, it was just that…well…suddenly his pancakes didn't feel so special if she was making food for all of them. He watched in confusion as Elise set her brown bag of treats upon the only cleared space on the worktable.

"You made *everyone* their own cookies?" Unfortunately, the bulldozer engine shut down right as he'd opened his mouth, making his accusation come out way louder than he'd intended.

"Why are you shouting like someone stole your cordless drill, boss?" Buster's knowing smile was barely discernable behind his heavy mustache and long beard. "You thought you were the only one Miss Mack cooked for?"

Harris crossed his arms in front of his chest. "No, of course not. I just figured Elise is already busy enough with her full-time job plus the work at the Maple Street property and now helping us out over here. She doesn't need to be taking custom cookie orders and worrying about who doesn't want cinnamon, which isn't even a real allergy by the way."

"It makes me sneeze." Buster's shrug caused him to drop the sledgehammer. Which conveniently freed up both of his hands so he could pry off the lid of the container Elise was handing him.

"Maybe it's the way that you inhale your food that makes you sneeze," Harris suggested as his barrel-chested foreman shoved an entire cookie into his mouth. "You should try taking a breath when you eat to see if that helps."

"I made you some, too, Harris." Elise handed him his own plastic container filled with freshly baked goodness, which only slightly appeased him. At least she hadn't forgotten about him altogether. Before he could turn them into a mess of crumbs like Buster had, she handed him a thick folder, as well. "I also brought some pictures of a few ideas I had for the siding colors and trim. Although, when I drove by yesterday afternoon, I didn't realize that you were going to get rid of the entire porch."

"We weren't," Buster said around another mouthful of cookie. "But then Harris fell right through some boards that had so much termite damage we thought there had to be all kinds of nasty bugs and creepy-crawlies living underneath the thing."

Harris shivered at the memory but didn't want Elise thinking the whole place was infested. She'd never want to step foot inside. He gave Buster a pointed look. "It wasn't *that* bad under there."

"That's not what you were saying when you were stuck waist-deep and hollering about something crawling up your pant leg, boss." Buster clearly had no idea of when to shut up. "I was laughing so hard I kept dropping my crowbar. Miguel was tossing patio furniture every which way because he thought we were gonna need to bring in the bucket to get Harris out. But the boss thought that'd take too long. Tony and Owen had to grab him under the armpits and yank him outta there before he screamed the whole roof down."

"I've noticed that Harris has an aversion to feral animals, so I can only imagine how he must feel about…what did you call them?" Elise might have been talking to Buster, but her eyes were full of laughter as she watched Harris. "Creepy-crawlies?"

"Make fun of me all you want." Harris fought the urge to shudder by keeping his arms defiantly crossed. "But most people would react the same way I did when threatened with the likelihood of being eaten alive. Both times."

This caused Elise and Buster to break out into a fit of giggles and Harris would've been annoyed that the joke was at his expense if he hadn't enjoyed watching Elise laugh like this.

When she finally drew a ragged breath and wiped the tear out of her eye, she saw Harris watching her. The humor slowly faded from her expression, and she focused on the house behind him. "Anyway, I was hoping I could get a feel for the interior layout before I start sketching some ideas."

"Right." She was here for a tour of the house. Not to provide a milk-and-cookies break or to swap stories about Harris's very rational fear of wild creatures. "Let me grab an extra hard hat for you out of the truck. We've already started demo and Buster's been living up to his nickname. It might not be structurally sound in there just now."

He jogged over to his truck, which was still chained to the old tree trunk they'd needed to pull up in order to tear out the now nonexistent front steps. When he returned with the white reinforced plastic hat, he heard his foreman saying, "So that's why they call me Buster. Nobody can bust through a wall as fast as me. Hey, Harris, Miss Mack was just telling me she doesn't have a nickname. We'll have to find something that fits."

Harris didn't point out that Miss Mack *was* a nickname. Or that he sometimes slipped and called her Lise. He might have to share her cookies with everyone else, but he didn't have to share that.

Whoa.

It was one thing to get jealous over some cinnamon-free baked goods. It was quite another to feel as though he had some sort of special right or privilege when it came to Elise. Obviously, she could do whatever she wanted with whomever she wanted. He didn't have any claim to her.

Still.

It was a little annoying that Buster was following them around as they toured the house. In fact, the foreman did most of the talking and Elise quietly nodded or sometimes made a note on a pad of lined paper she carried with her. If it had been anyone else, Harris would've wanted to be the one to explain his vision. To show off his plans for turning this rundown house into another financial success. However, he found himself wanting to watch her instead. He wanted to see what she was seeing and experience it through her eyes.

He also didn't want to make the same mistake he'd made with the flirty real estate agent—talking so much and so excitedly that he didn't take the time to read the room and gauge Elise's expectations.

They'd gone through the entire house and had returned to the ground floor before she finally asked a question. "How hard would it be to convert this powder room into a full bathroom?"

"You mean like add a shower or a tub?" Buster asked. "I guess if you wanted to knock out this wall and lose the coat closet in the hallway, you could do it. But why? There's already two full ones upstairs, plus the master bath."

Harris had a feeling he knew where she was going with this, but he forced himself to be patient. He wanted to hear if her thoughts matched up with his own. He also just wanted to hear *her*, to hear her voice, to hear her excitement when she latched on to a subject and lost all sense of shyness as she rambled on and on about it.

"Well, there's both a living room and a family room down here already. I know you wanted to make the den a home office, but if I were working from home, I'd rather be up there on one of the third floor cupolas, with windows looking out in all directions. So my suggestion would be to turn this area—the den and powder room— into a downstairs guest suite. We lived in a house similar to this when I was a girl and as my dad got older and his knees started bothering him, I remember watching him struggle to walk up the steps. More and more families are becoming multigenerational and have a senior relative living with them. If you provide access to a walk-in shower on the ground floor, you can still give the buyer the option of what they want to do with the space."

Harris chuckled, glad he'd waited for her explanation. "Okay, I thought you were going to suggest a pet washing station, but this actually makes more sense. There *is* a growing demand for ground-level master suites and—" he opened the door to the hall closet and ran his hand along the back wall "—the plumbing to the kitchen is already running through here. It's definitely doable. What else are you thinking?"

"So, the dining room is closed off with a boxy entry point. The ceilings are tall enough that we could open it up a little more with a wide arch. That chandelier is a work of art, but it's off-center. The wiring box should be moved about a foot to the left. The bricks around the fireplace are a bit too orange and don't all match. I think we can white-wash them and add a wood mantle to keep it looking rustic, like a farmhouse instead of a 1980s pizza oven. Then there's the awkward hallway between the family room and the back patio. It makes no sense functionality-wise since you could knock it out and have direct access with a set of French doors, adding more space and more light."

She took a deep breath, which Harris knew was only a brief pause before she began the second half of whatever she was going to say. But Buster didn't give her the time to continue.

The grinning foreman was already pulling on his work gloves. "Sounds like I'm gonna get to bust down a lot more walls."

"The only thing getting busted around here is my budget," Harris muttered to himself.

Unfortunately, Elise heard him.

Her mouth formed a little O and she blinked several times, all the joy and confidence vanishing from her expression in the blink of an eye. "Of course, we don't have to do any of that. Obviously, it all costs money and I'm sure that'll cut into the profits. I was just kind of thinking out loud. Forget I mentioned anything."

"No. All your suggestions are really fantastic ideas that will probably make the company much more money in the long run." Harris mentally kicked himself for his smart-aleck comment because the last thing he wanted to do was make Elise doubt herself. "This is the reason why I hired you. I need someone to keep things fresh. To challenge me."

"*I* challenge you," Buster pointed out.

Harris rolled his eyes. "I mean in a productive way, not in an annoying big brother way. So, Lise, what are your thoughts on paint colors and flooring?"

See. *There* was her nickname.

"Well, speaking of fresh." Elise bit her lower lip, less confident than she'd been before. Harris nodded, hoping to encourage her. "I went online and looked at some of the houses you've sold recently and, um, the thing is… Well, they all have the same color front door and the same bathroom tiles and there's just not much variation. Is that some sort of branding idea, like a signature design you want to keep standard in all the houses you flip?"

"No. In fact, I'd prefer to have things stand out rather than blend in." He saw something flicker in her eyes, almost as though she'd just winced. He was about to ask her what was wrong, but Buster reminded them both of his presence.

"Ever since Adina left, the boss has been playing it safe with his tried-and-true methods. As much as he likes to think he's the creative sort, he tends to follow his same patterns. And not just on the job. He eats the same food all the time. Dates the same kind of women too." A loud crash sounded outside, and Buster let out a curse. "I better go check and see what they broke out there."

Harris watched her shift from one foot to the other, which was what she did whenever she was about to run away. Although, recently he'd realized she did it less often. That had to be some sort of progress. Yet she was clearly uncomfortable about something. She still had twenty minutes before she had to be at Barkyard Boarding, but maybe she was worried about being late.

"So like my overopinionated foreman told you,"

Harris said, wanting to put her at ease. "It is definitely time for me to change things up a bit."

"Some people might argue that by moving on from one remodeling project to the next, you *are* changing things up. At least as far as your work patterns go." Elise shrugged, then focused her gaze on a spot behind him. "Of course, I can't speak to whether you move on from one thing to the next as far as your...uh...social patterns go."

"I guess I do." Harris chuckled thinking of the text he'd gotten from one of his buddies earlier. "Ian sent me a message this morning asking if I wanted to meet at Pins and Pints today for lunch. But I've already eaten there twice this week, so I suggested we hit Main Street Grille instead. He asked why it mattered since I was just going to order a double bacon cheeseburger anyway. But not every restaurant makes it the same way."

"What happened to the Vega family motto of taking a chance?"

"That's more for the bigger, life-altering decisions. I try not to waste my time fixing things that aren't broken."

Her eyes narrowed. "So when it comes to work, dating and eating, you just go from one place to the next, trying out different versions of the same thing?"

"I mean, sometimes I take a chance on onion rings instead of fries."

"How unpredictable of you." Elise's tone held the slightest note of sarcasm, but she quickly turned the page on her notepad and started walking toward the open front door and the demolished front porch. "So what are your thoughts on expanding this entryway?"

Ten minutes later, Buster let out a low whistle as Elise drove away. "She certainly isn't your usual type."

"Tell me about it." Harris nodded. "I know she doesn't have the same résumé as Adina, but you heard her ideas in there. I like that she sees the function of the space as much as the design."

"No, I meant she's not like the gals you usually date."

"Elise?" Harris whipped his head toward the stocky foreman. "I'm not dating her."

"Not yet, you're not. But it's pretty obvious you want to."

"Don't be ridiculous." Harris added a snort of disbelief for good measure, realizing after the fact that it only made him sound more defensive. "Besides, even if I *was* interested in her, she has a lot going on in her life right now. Including keeping your and everyone else's cookie orders straight, apparently. She probably doesn't have time to think about dating someone let alone bringing up the topic... Oh crap."

Buster lifted a dark eyebrow with a scar down the middle of it.

"She actually asked about my social life, but I didn't realize she was referring to relationships, specifically." Harris gave the foreman a pointed look. "It was right after you brought up the fact that I always dated the same type of women."

"So I opened up the discussion for you. You're welcome. Did you tell her you were currently single?"

"Nope. I stood there like an idiot and talked about cheeseburgers."

Chapter Six

Elise tried not to think about Harris as she drove by Main Street Grille on her way home from work later that afternoon. But her windows were down and the aroma of sizzling beef and grilled onions nearly convinced her to pull into the restaurant and experience the bacon cheeseburgers for herself.

No. She needed to save her money.

Besides, she'd just end up siting there staring at the menu and thinking about Harris casually joking that he sometimes changed things up by swapping out the fries for the rings.

Elise sank lower in her seat. That whole conversation had been so awkward. Most likely, he'd just been talking about actual food and not actually referring to the women he dated. Yet she couldn't stop herself from wondering which menu item *she* was most like. Probably something simple and useful and dull that usually got overlooked, like a side salad.

Not that she was a side piece. A side *dish*, she quickly corrected herself.

Ugh. Pushing her foot down on the accelerator, she sped by the restaurant, wanting to get all thoughts of Harris Vega out of her mind.

This was the problem with being an introvert and not having much dating experience. Elise was a twenty-five-year-old woman in the prime of her life. She should be going out with friends or pursuing hobbies—having fun and enjoying new experiences. Instead, she was driving around town in her ancient minivan, her plain work shirt covered in cat hair and dog slobber, while equating relationships to restaurant food.

"Not that I'd have it any other way." Elise smiled at her tired reflection in the review mirror, feeling more like herself than she had in the past ten years.

She was making her own money, living her own life and finally out of her aunt's shadow. It was Friday night, and she could do whatever she wanted, with whomever she wanted. It just so happened that she wanted to go home and shower, eat a PB and J, and then get to work on the web page for the cutest pets contest.

Luckily, Shane didn't mind Elise working on the Furever Paws fundraiser when she wasn't busy during her shifts. He'd even agreed to keep a stack of flyers at the reception desk.

He'd also been flexible about her shifting around some of her working hours. Now that the college kids had returned to the university for the fall semester, Shane had hired a few of them on a part-time basis to cover the weekend shifts. That allowed Elise to spend Saturday working on the Maple Street house and Sunday researching and sketching design ideas for her first-ever remodel project.

Which was exactly what she did. She threw herself into all her tasks that weekend with such gusto, she hardly had any free time to think of Harris. She also barely had time to go to the grocery store and start her meal prepping for the upcoming week.

Barely.

She was standing in her driveway, unloading groceries from the back of her car when she heard the yipping behind her. A gravity defying bolt of brown leaped into her trunk area and immediately began nosing into the contents of the produce bags.

"Hello, there, Mr. Frankfurter." She gently lifted the wily, but otherwise friendly dachshund who lived across the street. "Did you escape your leash again?"

Roxy Cole, the sixteen-year-old owner, was out of breath when she jogged into the driveway, a smartphone in one hand and an empty collar still attached to the leash in the other.

"Hey, Roxy," Elise said as the teen approached. "Did you try using the halter I brought you from work?"

"I can't get Mr. Frank to sit still long enough to put it on him. As soon as he sees me grab my running shoes, he starts barking his head off and doing laps around the living room."

"Yeah. They can sense when it's time for a walk." Elise gently pried the dark green peel out of Mr. Frankfurter's mouth. "Or when there's food nearby."

"Sorry," Roxy said as she typed on her phone. "I'll check and see if we have an extra avocado at home since he just ate yours."

"That's okay. I still have one more." But the girl made no move to take the now-squirming dog. In fact, she frowned as she used two fingers to zoom in and out on her phone. Elise shifted Mr. Frankfurter high in her arms and asked, "Is everything alright?"

"No, it's not. My boyfriend said he couldn't hang out today because he has to work on an essay for AP English." Roxy held up her screen, showing Elise a picture on social media. "But his best friend just posted this. They're clearly hanging out at the Whole Bean."

"But they *do* have their laptops in the picture," she said to the scowling teen, who zoomed in and out of the image as though searching for some sort of clue. "And that coffee place has really good Wi-Fi."

"But do you see the barista working behind the counter? That's Holly Fitzsimmons. Last year, the entire girls varsity volleyball team shipped Holly and Brandon."

"Shipped them where?" Elise asked, giving the dachshund a small piece of avocado to prevent him from diving into another grocery bag.

"No." Roxy rolled her eyes. "Ship is short for relationship. When you get shipped with someone, it means people think you'd make a cute couple. Brandon *claimed* he didn't like Holly, and that's why he asked me out instead."

"That's good, right?" Elise asked, hoping she didn't sound as naive as she felt. Or as archaic, considering she was less than a decade older than the teen. "Brandon chose you. I don't think you have anything to worry about with Holly."

"Then why isn't he responding to any of my messages?" Roxy asked, as though her unattached and introverted new neighbor, who hadn't had a date in years, could give her some reassuring advice. "Did you ever have a boyfriend when you were my age, Miss Elise?"

Oh great. She looked up and down the street to

see if there was anyone else more qualified to have this conversation with a teenage girl in obvious distress. But not even nosy Reverend Johnson was peeking out his window. Elise was all on her own.

The closest thing she'd had to a boyfriend had been Carter, a physical therapist who worked at her dad's assisted living center. The first three years John Mackenzie had been at Horizons, Regina had only taken her niece sporadically to visit him. After Elise turned eighteen and got her driver's license, though, she started visiting weekly. But by then, her dad usually had no idea who she was. Fortunately, Carter could always make her dad smile, and Elise's visits with the older man were better when the physical therapist was working. Pretty soon, she and Carter became friends and then started going out to eat after his shifts.

"I…um…didn't really start dating until I was a couple of years older than you," Elise finally answered. "There was this one guy I was sort of seeing. As soon as my aunt found out about us, she… uh…put a stop to it."

Actually, Regina had become quite livid, ranting about having Carter fired for fraternizing with a patient's family.

Roxy tilted her head. "But you were already eighteen? How could your aunt tell you what to do?"

"Looking back, I'm starting to ask myself that

same thing." Regina had been very controlling over Elise's life. She'd always said that it was because she cared, because she was looking out for her niece since she was the only family Elise had left. Maybe that was true. She wanted to believe it was. But lately…she'd started to have some doubts. And even if Regina really had been well-intentioned, that didn't mean that every choice she made was right. It was getting harder and harder to believe there could be any innocent, reasonable explanation for her leaving town with Furever Paws's money.

"I guess I'd been living with my aunt for so long, it just became easier to keep the peace and do whatever she wanted. Besides, my dad was really sick, and she was the one paying for all his medical bills. I didn't want to seem ungrateful."

"That sucks. What about the guy? What did he say to your aunt?"

"That's a good question." The next time Elise had gone to visit her father, Carter had been gone. "I have no idea. I tried texting him and even called him once, but it went straight to voicemail. He never responded."

Roxy gasped. "You mean he ghosted you?"

"I guess you could say that. Except, in his defense, my aunt *did* have him fired from his job."

"Your aunt sounds like a real controlling Asshole, with a capital *A*." The assessment should have been shocking coming from someone so young.

However, finally hearing another person say it aloud was also somewhat liberating. While Elise felt the knee-jerk impulse to defend her aunt, she decided this time to swallow it down.

Instead, she smiled weakly at Roxy. "You might be right."

"But also, what kind of guy doesn't tell your aunt to shove off and go find a different job? If you ask me, he should've fought for you."

Before Elise could ponder that observation, Roxy's phone rang and she immediately swiped her finger across the screen to answer it. "Oh, hey, Brandon. Did you have a good time hanging out with Holly?"

"I wasn't hanging out with her," came the male voice on the other end. Did all teenagers talk in public on FaceTime? Elise wanted to give them privacy, but technically they were on her property. Plus, she couldn't just walk away with Roxy's dog, nor did it seem like a good idea to set him loose. She had no choice but to stand there and hear Brandon fire back, "I was working on my paper. Why are you freaking out?"

"I'm not freaking out," Roxy said with a surprisingly calm tone for someone who had in fact been freaking out a few minutes ago. "I was just chilling with Elise, talking about how men can be so weak and would rather avoid a simple phone call than just be honest about what they're doing."

Ouch. That hadn't exactly been the focal point of their conversation. Had it?

"Who's Elise?" Brandon asked.

"My really good friend." Roxy aimed the phone in Elise's direction and then back so quickly, she only had enough time to catch a glimpse of the teenage boy in the baseball cap. "Her car is practically a party bus and can fit, like, a whole bunch of the girls when we go out."

Elise whipped her head toward the interior of the minivan that absolutely nobody on earth would ever consider a party bus. She whispered, "I really don't think there's enough seat belts for something like that."

However, Roxy flipped her hair as she kept talking to Brandon. "Also, Elise is over twenty-one, so she can buy us alcohol too. Unlike your brother's friend who got his fake ID confiscated last month at the liquor store."

This time, Elise's whisper was even more forceful. "I'm not buying anyone alcohol."

Roxy waved her off. "Not that I'd even go drinking and risk getting kicked off the cross-country team. Because some of us, Brandon, understand that there's consequences for our actions."

"What actions?" The boy argued. "I didn't even talk to Holly. I did nothing wrong."

"Well, I'm sure that didn't stop *her* from giving you a free pumpkin scone with your caramel latte," Roxy accused as she turned toward her own house, the empty collar still dangling from the leash in her free hand.

"Geez, Rox. Holly actually gave Cortez the scone because *he's* the one who has the crush on her. I was just there as his wingman. And to write my AP paper."

"Braaaandon," the girl squealed with sudden excitement. "You didn't tell me Cortez liked her. That makes total sense, though. I'd totally ship them. Do you think we should see if they want to go with us to homecoming? Did I tell you about my dress yet?"

"Uh, Roxy?" Elise called out, lifting the dachshund higher in her arms. "You forgot Mr. Frankfurter."

But the teenager was halfway across the street, her earlier anger at her boyfriend now forgotten as she gushed about heels versus flats and the best places to take pictures before the dance.

"Well, little guy," Elise told the dog in her arms. "You want to come inside and help me meal prep?"

The animal whipped its pointy tail happily, likely because he knew he'd get to clean up the kitchen floor every time she dropped a bit of food. For the next three hours, Elise chopped and measured and stirred and packaged and talked to a tiny-legged dog as though she were in a therapy session.

"I know you can't tell, but I'm actually putting myself out there a lot more than I used to," she told

Mr. Frankfurter. "I mean, I have two jobs now, and I'm kind of starting to enjoy the people I work with. Some more than others. Of course, I'm still having a hard time reading people. For instance, Roscoe's owner kept telling me to stop by her salon and she'd hook me up with a haircut. I think she was implying that she won't charge me, or that she at least plans on giving me a discount. I mean, her Saint Bernard has this intense drooling problem, and I was the one who came up with the neck kerchief that doubles as slobber bib. So maybe she thinks she owes me? But what if I assume wrong and then get to her salon and have to pay full price for some hairstyle I don't even want?"

Elise slid a tray of zucchini muffins out of the oven. "Okay, that's the last batch. I guess I have nothing left to cook except the pancakes. Except, if I start working on Harris's pancakes, then I'll start thinking about him again. And I've done a really good job of keeping him out of my mind all weekend."

The dachshund plopped himself in front of the table. With his hind legs stretched out behind him and his two front paws extended out to his sides, he looked like an airplane gliding in for a landing.

"You're right. It's time for me to be spreading my wings too. Not just at work, but maybe relationship-wise? Maybe I should get a dating app on my phone and just, sort of, see what's out there.

I'm sure Harris Vega isn't the only guy in the world who can pique my interest."

Elise stood there, staring at the ingredients for pancakes as she thought about the types of men she might meet. Wait. What if they'd heard about her aunt? She didn't have to tell anyone her last name did she? Maybe she could find someone who would rather eat than talk. But then what if they didn't like her cooking? Or what if they didn't like her? Harris knew her last name *and* seemed to like both her and her cooking. But maybe he was just being friendly.

The problem was that Elise's body didn't exactly react in a friendly way whenever she was around him. Her insides got all warm and gooey, like that bottle of maple syrup near the stove. Then her hands would get fidgety and she'd talk way too fast to stop herself from imagining how he'd look without his work shirt on, wearing nothing but his jeans and his tool belt.

Mr. Frankfurter's ears perked up and he made a little growl.

"Don't worry," Elise told the dog. "Even if he *were* to ask me out, it's not like I could actually date him. He's my boss. And my landlord. Can you imagine how messy that could become? Besides, unlike him, I'm not the type to rush into things."

The dachshund responded with a protective bark, and it was then that she heard a meow in the distance. "Oh, you're not warning me off Harris Vega.

You're just reminding me it's time to feed the cats. See that's just one more reason why I shouldn't be thinking about dating anyone. With everything going on in my life, when would I even find the time?"

"I think we should keep the faucet, as well," Elise told Harris the following Thursday evening. The rest of the crew had left and it was just the two of them at the colonial on Dawson Avenue. "It's so beautiful and it fits in perfectly with that antique rustic theme we're trying to maintain throughout the house."

He leaned over the wide farmhouse sink she'd already insisted on keeping when they'd torn out all the kitchen cabinets. But none of his attention was on the faucet in front of his face. He was too busy finishing the last of the red velvet cupcakes she'd brought for Tony's birthday.

"It's not that I don't agree with you, Lise," he finally replied as he brushed some crumbs from his mouth. "At least, not from a design standpoint. It's just that most of the lead pipes will need to be replaced and an old fixture like this won't be able to handle the modern updates."

She had a pencil tucked behind her ear and a tape measure clipped to the belt loop of her jeans. Wow, her waist really was tiny. Harris was pretty sure he could span his two hands around it. He flexed his fingers before noticing a smear of cream cheese frosting still on them. He licked it clean.

Elise gulped. "Could you please not do that?"

"Do what?" he asked, using his tongue on his thumb, as well. Was she upset that he'd pushed back on her faucet plan? All week long he'd listened to her good ideas and hadn't said no to many of them. In fact, he'd been pretty impressed with how organized her lists were and how much research she'd done whenever she'd suggested implementing various design elements. He hoped his comment about the old pipes hadn't come across as dismissive or mansplaining.

She closed her eyes and gave a little shake of her head, dislodging the pencil and a loose curl. "You're distracting me while I'm trying to focus."

How was he distracting...? Oh. A zing of awareness shot through him. Wow. Apparently, Elise was just as preoccupied by him as he was by her. That was good to know. Suddenly the frosting tasted all the sweeter and he couldn't hold back his grin. "So I make you lose focus?"

"No, the cupcake makes me lose focus. I skipped lunch today because one of the dog trainers got a flat tire and I offered to change it for him. But his spare was also pretty low on air, so I covered the one o'clock Puppy and Me class while he took it in to get fixed."

"Wow. Changing tires and running classes.

You're proving to be quite the asset over there at Barkyard Boarding."

"Anyone would've done the same." Her tone held her usual trace of humility, but she lifted her chin a little higher, the pride written all over her face.

"Speaking of your assets." Harris's eyes inadvertently dipped lower to her hips for just a second before he commanded them back up. "When I stopped by the feed store a couple of days ago to buy more Feline Finest, the owner mentioned that you'd talked him into donating several gift cards and a silent auction basket for the fundraiser at Furever Paws."

"Yeah. I had to promise him that we'd use his company logo on the backdrop banner for the fashion show. His competitor across town wasn't exactly thrilled to get upstaged, so she bought a corporate sponsorship and then donated a bunch of promotional chew toys to the swag bags all the guests will be taking home."

"Corporate sponsorships and swag bags. Well played. Your dad would be very proud of your salesmanship."

At that, Elise did duck her head, her proud smile replaced by a modest grin.

"It's okay to take a compliment, you know." Harris used his finger to lift Elise's chin. As her wide brown eyes searched his face, he realized that if he took one step closer to her, he'd risk drowning in their depths. "This newfound confidence looks good on you, Elise Mackenzie."

She blinked once, twice, then tilted up one corner of her mouth. "If it's confidence you want, then I'm pretty confident that this faucet will be just fine staying right where it belongs."

Now Harris rolled *his* eyes because he was equally confident that it wouldn't work. "They have plenty of retro-looking replicas we could get that would be way better with the modern plumbing. Besides, the spigot comes directly out of the wall and once we cut the plaster out of the way, there's no doubt going to be some serious mildew and condensation issues back there."

"Why waste money on a replica when the real deal is already right here and we can use flexible supply tubes with some compression couplings to link it to the new pipes?" Elise helped herself to a flathead screwdriver out of his tool belt, reminding him of the first time they'd been at the cat colony and she'd grabbed the keys from his pocket. Except this time, she seemed way more at ease. She scraped the pointy edge of the tool along the base flange. "Look how sturdy it is."

As if to prove her point, she tapped the screwdriver to the cold water tap and just like that, the old pewter knob busted right off and water exploded at them.

Well, mostly at Elise since she was the one standing directly in the path of the powerful spray. Her startled shriek forced Harris to spring into action and he dove in front of her, first using his hands to redirect the force of the stream, and then his entire body to block her.

"I thought Buster shut off the water to the house," he yelled over the groaning pipes. "Can you go check the main valve? It's outside behind the garage."

Elise sprinted through the back door and Harris wrestled with the buttons of his wet work shirt. He needed to redirect the gushing water downward and into the sink before the runoff raced across the kitchen floor and toward the stacks of brand-new drywall the crew had left piled near the butler's pantry.

He was using the wadded shirt as a funnel of sorts when Elise ran back in. "The valve handle is rusted in place. Did you check under the sink for a secondary?"

"No, I've kinda got my hands full trying to save those stacks of drywall over there from ending up in a pool of water."

"I'll find it!" Elise vanished from his peripheral vision and for a second, he had no idea where she'd gone. Until he felt something brush against his inner calf.

"Please tell me that's you," Harris yelled, trying

to hold his position as a human dam while someone—or something—crawled between his boots.
"And not that fat possum Buster found living in
the attic."

"Buster said the possum wasn't *that* big." He
took his eyes off the haphazardly funneled spray
long enough to glance down and see Elise on her
hands and knees below him, her head now hidden
under the sink. He widened his stance to allow her
better access, wondering how long he could hold
this awkward position. Just when he thought he
was going to need to shift his weight, she yelled,
"Got it!"

The water stopped and Harris let the soaking ball
of flannel drop into the sink. Elise tried to back out
from the tunnel between his legs at the exact same
moment he lifted his right knee to step over her.
Her elbow slammed into his left shin and Harris
scrambled to reach the edge of the sink to regain
his balance. Unfortunately, his wet hand couldn't
grip on the slippery porcelain.

He heard Elise's muffled *oompf* right as he
landed on his butt in a puddle on the hardwood
floor. She was beside him, sprawled on her stomach with his right leg pinning down the back of
her thighs.

Crap.

"Are you okay?" He winced at the pain shooting through his tailbone as he twisted toward her.

Her hair was dripping wet and covering her face, so all he could see were her shoulders shaking. Was she crying? Was she injured? Why didn't she answer him?

"Lise?" Since he had no idea if she'd broken a bone in the collision, Harris resisted the frantic urge to flip her over and check for injuries. Instead, his fingers pushed the damp strands from her cheeks, mentally bracing himself for the pain he might see reflected in her eyes.

What he hadn't expected to witness was Elise nearly choking on laughter. Keeping his hand in place, he dropped his head to the ground in relief. The loud wet *thunk* only made Elise laugh harder.

"Well, I'm glad I could bring some amusement to your evening," he said, unable to hold back his own chuckle. Her giggles were contagious and, well, he could only imagine how ridiculous they must both look, lying there like a couple of drenched rag dolls that had washed up to shore.

He shifted to his hip and groaned.

"Oh no, Harris." Elise's face sobered quickly. "Are you hurt?"

He reached below him to yank free the source of his discomfort. "No, I just rolled onto your tape measure."

This started another round of suppressed giggles that soon turned into full-fledged belly laughs. At some point, one of her hands fell across his bicep and she held on to him as though they were the only two people left in the world.

At the moment, it kind of felt as if they were.

Her head was tipped back, her eyes squeezed shut and her mouth wide open as she sucked in air between bursts of laughter. Harris had never seen a more beautiful sight. Or a more inviting one.

He suddenly ached all over, but not because of the fall.

Remaining on his side, he slowly angled his face until it was just inches away from hers. Kissing her might scare her off, but he couldn't stop himself from moving in closer, wanting to physically absorb all the joy bursting from her. Reaching across her body, he braced his left hand on the hardwood floor beside her waist, planting it on the solid ground rather than the soft curve of her body. How about that for impulse control?

As he shifted over her, Elise's palm slid from his bicep to his chest. Despite the damp cotton of his T-shirt, he felt the heat from her splayed fingers explode across his pectoral muscle.

The laughter slowly subsided, and her eyes went from playful to curious as she examined his face. Somewhere in the back of his brain, he knew he should push himself up and offer to get her a towel or something. If he didn't act quickly to remind them both of their professional boundaries, then this moment could change everything. Yet that warning was drowned out by the pounding of his heart as Elise brought her hand to the nape of his neck and gently pulled his head toward hers.

Chapter Seven

As he'd lingered over her, Elise had watched Harris's thoughts play out across his face. His playful grin had eased into a satisfied smirk before disappearing completely. Then his nostrils flaring slightly as her thumb moved across his wet T-shirt, accidentally grazing his hardened nipple. The dark shadow of stubble along his lower cheeks couldn't disguise the restraint of his clenched jaw. She might not have much experience with guys, but she saw the exact moment in his eyes when he was about to do the honorable thing and pull away from her. He was a good man, a protective man who might walk a flirtatious line, but he would never step across it uninvited.

In that case, consider him invited.

She brought his mouth down to hers, the vibration of his groan against her lips making her buzz with both pleasure and a keen sense of recklessness. Harris was clearly more skilled in this department than she was, yet he followed her lead. Even though she was below him, Elise had never felt more powerful. Her fingers dived into his hair, angling his head only slightly so that she could deepen the kiss.

She set a slow and leisurely pace as her tongue explored his mouth and her hands explored everywhere else. Harris held himself still for the most part, only shifting his body weight to allow her better access as her palms moved lower down his torso.

A few minutes ago, already numbingly cold from going outside in her wet clothes, she'd been frozen in place when she'd reentered the kitchen and seen Harris standing there in his soaked white tee, his lithe muscles on display under the now-transparent fabric. Now, though, she could swear there was steam rising between them as their heated bodies pressed together.

Suddenly, Elise wanted more than steam. She wanted fire. Grabbing a fistful of damp cotton, her knuckles grazed against his bare skin as she peeled the hem of Harris's shirt away from his body. She was so focused on completing her task without breaking their kiss, she didn't hear the ringing at first.

Neither did he, apparently, because she was the first to respond to it. Reluctantly, she pulled her mouth away from his, practically panting before drawing in a deep breath. "Do you need to answer that?"

His eyes blinked open, and he slowly retreated until she could no longer hear those sexy deep sighs coming from the back of his throat. All she could hear was the incessant shrill of his annoyingly loud ringtone.

"Sorry." He winced as he reached for the phone clipped to his belt. "I put it on the highest setting when we were doing demo. How long has it been going off?"

Elise bit back a satisfied smile at the realization that their recent fog of passion had deafened him to outside sounds more effectively than Buster's jackhammer.

Harris squinted at the screen. "I'm going to need to take this. Excuse me for a sec."

"Hello," he answered as he rose to his feet. But instead of leaving, he reached down with his free hand to help Elise stand while he listened attentively to the person on the other end of the line.

Not that Elise was eavesdropping, but his phone volume was still loud enough that she could tell it was a woman's voice speaking to him. She just couldn't understand what they were saying. Soon the only thing she could hear were the alarm bells inside her head when she realized Harris was standing there completely shirtless.

Looking away quickly, Elise caught a glimpse of her water-logged appearance in the reflection of the window above the sink. Oh no. She had way more important things to tend to rather than listening to his conversation or trying to remember what she'd done with his shirt. First and foremost was the mess of tangled wet hair that had escaped its elastic holder.

"It's okay, Maggie," Harris said, and Elise's gaze jumped, their eyes meeting in the window's reflection. "I can stop by there on my way home."

He was now close enough to Elise that she could hear whoever Maggie was say, "I hope I'm not interrupting your night."

"Don't worry about it," Harris replied casually while winking at Elise.

But instead of her usual heated blush, all Elise could feel was an icy chill.

Was it jealousy that he was talking to another woman? Elise certainly didn't have any claim to the man. Was it mortification at the possibility that she'd misread his interest in her? Maybe. Except the fly of his jeans still strained against the evidence of his earlier arousal. There was no denying that he'd responded to her. But now the moment was over and she wasn't sure what would happen next.

Her first instinct was to get out of the house before he got off the phone and they had to pretend that what occurred five minutes ago was a totally random accident that would never happen again. Or worse. Pretend like it never happened at all.

But her second instinct was to avoid driving home wet in the cool night air. If Elise came down with a nasty cold, she didn't have any extra money to waste on a co-pay for the doctor.

She had a sweatshirt in her car, along with some running clothes she'd changed into at work since they were boarding a whippet this week who needed more exercise than a usual walk. While Harris was busy telling Maggie that he had nothing better to do with his evening than go see to whatever it was she needed, Elise turned and headed toward the front door.

"Where are you going?" Harris whispered, his hand cupped around the speaker of his phone.

"I have to go get something from my car," she replied, not bothering to lower her voice.

It wasn't as though she and Harris had actual plans tonight, Elise reminded herself as she hurried outside. *She* was the one who'd surprised him with the kiss. In fact, she hadn't thought much beyond that moment. If the phone hadn't interrupted them, would things have gone further between them?

Maybe Harris was relieved to have an excuse to leave before matters got any more complicated between them. Although, he hadn't seemed very relieved when he'd had to pull away from her and answer the call. He'd frowned in disappointment. Or so she'd thought at the time.

Elise's emotions wrestled inside her as she made her way to the car. One minute, she convinced herself that she was confident and had everything under control. The next minute, she found herself tumbling down the spiraling slope of self-doubt and awkwardness. Talking herself out of driving away for the second time in as many minutes, she retrieved her dry clothes then quickly bypassed the kitchen to go directly to the only room that still had a functioning door and lock—the upstairs master bathroom. If she moved fast enough, she could be changed and out of the house before Harris even noticed she was gone.

By the time she returned downstairs, feeling warmer and a bit less self-conscious, Harris was still on the phone. And he was still shirtless. "Good news, Maggie. They have the part for the water heater in stock. If I head over and pick it up now, I should have it installed before Cam and the twins get home for bath time."

Elise slapped her palm to her forehead, finally knocking loose her insecure assumptions about Harris. This was what happened when she overthought things.

No more thinking about the interrupted kiss, she commanded herself. No more thinking about anything. It was better to just say goodbye, and avoid the entire topic.

"See you soon." Harris disconnected the call before grabbing a canvas tarp off the work table and spreading it over the wet floor.

She rubbed her temples before plastering what she hoped was a convincing smile to her face. He was walking toward the stairway when he stopped in his tracks and did a double take at her.

"Wow. I thought I liked seeing you in jeans, but those tight exercise pants leave a lot less to the imagination."

Okay, so she most definitely *hadn't* imagined his interest in her. Something warm rekindled inside her. Instead of replying with an equally flirtatious comment, though, she said, "They're also covered in whippet hair because Johnny Rocket does laps around me when he thinks I'm not running fast enough on our jogs. But at least they're not drenching wet from rolling around in a puddle of water."

The second the words were out of her mouth, Elise wished she could pull them back in. So much for not bringing up the circumstances surrounding their earlier kiss.

"Good call. I should probably change out of

these wet clothes, too, before I head over to fix the water heater at one of my properties." Harris reached for where his shirt would have been if he'd been wearing one. Then his eyes darted to the dripping pile of cotton on the floor like it was no big deal that she'd practically torn the thing off him. "Looks like you already took care of part of that for me. I hope I still have a spare hoodie in the truck. One of my renters doesn't have any hot water and the rest of her family is coming home tonight from a three-day fishing trip. So if I don't get her water heater hose replaced soon, it's going to smell like river trout and dirty feet in her house for days."

Elise gulped at his casual reference to her being the one responsible for his current state of partial undress. Or maybe she was gulping at the sight of his bare arms and torso, his muscles lean and well formed with barely any dark hair sprinkled across his tan skin. Every time she thought she was coming to her senses, she realized she was getting closer and closer to the edge. It wouldn't take much before she crossed that point of no return.

Holding her gym bag in front of her as if it were a sort of shield that could protect her from danger, she slowly backed away from him, inching herself toward the door before she lost all willpower and self-respect. Just be cool. Pretend nothing is out of the ordinary.

"Well, I better hit the road so you can get going

to your next plumbing emergency," she offered right before bumping her shoulder into the door frame.

"Yeah, I seem to be having quite a few of those lately." He was most likely making a joke about the last two pipe issues she'd caused, but Elise couldn't be sure because she was desperately avoiding any sort of eye contact. "As soon as I get one project fixed up, another one comes along. Luckily, I like keeping my hands busy."

"Don't think about his hands," she murmured more to herself than to him.

"What's that?" he asked, but she had no intention of repeating it.

"Nothing. See you later." She gave an awkward wave before racing back to her car.

As she drove home, she couldn't stop touching her swollen lips or reliving the most intoxicating kiss of her life. She also couldn't stop the thought of how she may have just accidentally become one of Harris's projects.

Harris spent the next two weeks trying to come up with a plan for how to be alone with Elise again. He'd had a feeling that buried beneath Elise's reserved and shy personality there was a lot of passion and hidden depths just begging to be set free. He'd caught a glimmer of it when she talked about designing and cooking and animals, but the night they'd kissed, her intensity was beyond all of that combined. Unfortunately, he hadn't had another opportunity to experience it since then.

Anytime she came by the jobsite, it was always when most of the crew were still there. In addition to bringing a list of ideas or color samples, Elise always brought something she'd just whipped up in her kitchen, and everyone would sit around eating snacks and treats and sometimes entire meals instead of clocking out and going home like normal people do after a workday. Even Owen, whose wife made her world-famous meat loaf every Monday, went home late last night and ate his normal dinner as though he hadn't just shoved his face full of butterscotch blondies. The painter called in sick the following day with a belly ache, which meant it was only one less guy hanging around when Elise showed up Tuesday afternoon.

Some of the subcontractors from Harris's other jobsites now found reasons to stop by the colonial on Dawson Avenue around four thirty, as well. They'd figured out that was the usual time Elise would get there with that oversized tote bag she used for transporting her baked goods. Even if Harris caught a passing second with her in the half-gutted house, there was always someone on the other side of the studs hammering or plastering or yelling for a missing tool—or another mint chip brownie.

Surprisingly, she wasn't shy about asking any of the guys to help her implement her design ideas, and they seemed thrilled to find ways to accommodate her. Buster had spent an entire day driving around antique stores and hunting down a sliding barn door for the kitchen pantry after seeing a picture of what she had in mind. The crew had no problem giving her their opinions on her sample tiles or wallpaper swatches either. Of course, their opinions usually echoed her choices anyway.

But ever since their kiss, she never really talked to Harris one-on-one. And she certainly didn't make eye contact, unless she was asking him to approve a change in the budget. Even those requests were rare since she usually found ways to save money herself. It could be that she wasn't avoiding him so much as the woman was a constant whirlwind of activity. He had no idea how she managed to do everything.

Or it could be that she was one hundred percent avoiding him.

Hell, he couldn't even get her alone on the phone. When he closed escrow on a new house and asked if she wanted to meet after work on Thursday to do a walk-through with him, Elise created a group chat, inviting in Buster and offering to bring dinner to anyone there. So of course, all the guys showed up because who was going to turn down Elise's homemade fried chicken and chocolate cake? A few times, usually when Harris was busy eating her baked goods, he possibly caught her looking at him. But she was always quick to look away.

Maybe he needed a reason to go to her. She was always showing up with food and sketches of ideas, maybe he could take something to her for a change.

But what?

He kept asking himself that on Friday afternoon as he drove across town to his office. He needed to pick up the extra air ducting he'd ordered to accommodate Elise's walk-in closet addition. Even with the added paycheck from her design work, he had a feeling Elise's financial situation was pretty limited, especially considering how much she was likely spending in baking supplies. There were plenty of things he thought she needed—such as another pair of those snug running pants or a dozen notepads for all those handwritten lists she made. But she would be too proud to accept anything she thought she didn't need.

Pulling up to an intersection in front of the Corners strip mall, he thought about grabbing a burger from one of the food truck vendors parked in front of Pins and Pints and asking his buddy Calum Ramsey for an idea on what to get Elise. As he turned into the parking lot near the bowling alley, he saw another shop and knew exactly what he needed.

He was about to pull open the door to Chapter One Bookstore when he saw Calum walking that way. Harris nodded at the take-out container in his friend's hand. "If that's for me, you just saved me an extra stop."

"You wish." Calum grinned. "It's an order of habanero wings for Lucy. Extra spicy, which means I'm going to need to grab her a pint of gelato on my way home tonight. These pregnancy cravings are no joke."

"I can only imagine," Harris said honestly. Sure, he'd planned to get married and maybe have kids someday, but the thought didn't hold much urgency. Now that one of his best friends—a guy who nobody had expected to be the settling down type— was engaged and expecting a baby, "someday" no longer seemed as far into the future as it once had. "Family life looks good on you, man. I don't think I've seen you this happy since we were able to salvage that old mahogany bar when you bought the bowling alley three years ago."

"Find yourself the right woman—" Calum held open the door to the bookshop "—and you might look as good as me one day."

"Hey, Lucy," Harris greeted the very pregnant owner of Chapter One, who was stacking a pile of paperbacks on the counter next to the old-fashioned cash register. "Please tell your fiancé that I'm just as good-looking as him."

"Sorry, Harris." Lucy Tucker walked toward them and planted a kiss on Calum before taking the container of food. "Nobody could possibly be more handsome than the man who brings me habanero wings and rubs my feet at the end of a long week."

"Foot rubs too?" Harris lifted a brow.

"Best part of my day," Calum replied without a shred of embarrassment. In fact, the man seemed rather pleased with himself as he picked up a stuffed pumpkin and returned it to the Halloween-themed display in the huge picture window. "Where's Buttercup?"

The golden retriever must have heard her name because she lumbered slowly out of the back room and came to Calum before sniffing at his pocket, probably in the hopes of getting a treat.

"How're you doing, little mama?" His friend proved the dog's instincts right as he pulled out a napkin and uncovered a small morsel of meat. When she finished chewing, Calum patted her on the head. "Maybe before tonight's dinner rush, I can take you over to the shelter to visit your pups."

Buttercup must've liked that idea because her ears perked up and her tail swished back and forth.

"Just one pup, now," Lucy corrected, as she awkwardly bent down to straighten Buttercup's new collar. "Everyone but Pancake has been adopted. Because of that heart murmur, she's been a lot harder to place."

Harris felt like an outsider as he watched this happy little family who'd recently found each other.

Something tightened in his gut, and he experienced that same weird twinge he'd gotten when Elise had brought cookies for everyone else in his crew. This wasn't jealousy, though. It was envy. He wanted to be this happy with someone who—

"So what brings you in, Harris?" Lucy asked, interrupting his thoughts.

"Right." He was standing there daydreaming while this hungry, pregnant shop owner probably wanted to dive into her lunch. "I need to buy a book on plumbing. Preferably one that mentions antique faucets if you have one."

"Let me show you what we have in the household repairs section. If you don't see exactly what you're looking for in stock, we can do a search and I can order something in for you." Lucy tilted her head. "But it might be quicker for you to find a how-to video online."

"It's not for me. It's a gift for someone."

Calum narrowed his eyes. "I'd like to know who you think would want to unwrap a present and see a book about antique faucets."

"It's for Elise Mackenzie." Harris tried to shrug as though it was no big deal. But he couldn't stop the corners of his mouth from turning upward at the mention of her name. "And it's more of an inside joke than an actual gift."

"Is that right?" Calum's brow lifted with curiosity. "So you and your new tenant are taking things to the inside joke level, are you?"

One of the downsides to having a best friend who was a bartender was that Calum could read Harris just as easily as he could read any of the books in this shop.

"I'm not sure what level we're at." Harris might as well admit what was probably written all over his face. "At first we were just landlord and tenant. But things have been steadily progressing from there. She's doing some side work for me with designing and staging, so technically I guess I'm her boss, although she pretty much has the crew wrapped around her finger and we all do what she says. I'd like to think we're at the friend stage, if we haven't skipped right past it altogether. I'm definitely attracted to her, and it seems like she's attracted to me. But I don't want to push for something she may not be ready for."

"Nobody has ever accused you of being patient," Calum pointed out. "But I've found that it's best to just wait and see how things play out before rushing into anything when one or both of you might not be ready."

Lucy covered her smirk by biting into a piece of chicken. Calum had once confided in Harris that when he'd first found out she was expecting, he'd impulsively offered to marry her, almost out of a sense of duty. But Lucy had convinced Calum to wait until later in the pregnancy before making any decisions that he might regret. It had been a smart move on her part because it had given the couple time to realize that they had fallen in love and to accept that they wanted to be together regardless of the baby.

"I know." Harris rolled his shoulders and exhaled, as though he could prove just how relaxed he was about the whole situation. "Good things come to those who wait. It's frustrating, though, that I never took the time to get to know her before now. Elise is so smart and so funny when she forgets to be self-conscious. Every time I'm with her, I feel like I'm watching a butterfly slowly emerge from her cocoon. She has all these amazing ideas when it comes to designing the houses or to throwing this fundraiser for the animal rescue. The woman works nonstop, but she's so quiet and stealthy about it, you'd never notice. She's like a magical little fairy that does everything when nobody is looking. And don't even get me started on her cooking. I think I've gained five pounds since she's always bringing food to everyone on the jobsites."

"I'm sure your mom will be happy to know that you're eating more." Calum grinned and gave a little shake of his head. "Last time I saw Ms. Cindy she told me that a grown man needed to eat something besides bacon cheeseburgers."

Harris winced. "Yeah, maybe if you see Elise

around town, don't bring up the bacon cheeseburger thing. It's a long story, but I might've given her the impression that I have a certain type."

"A type of burger?" Lucy asked as she licked habanero sauce off her fingers. "Or a type of woman?"

"Both," Harris admitted as he rubbed the back of his neck. "Like I said, I'm trying to be patient and take things slowly. Remember that real estate agent when I first started out? How I was in such a rush to buy the house, I didn't read all the signs that she had something more than business in mind? Well, Elise is the opposite and the last thing I want to do is scare her off. Unfortunately, Buster already gave her the impression that I'm a bit of a player and that I always go after the same thing when it comes to dating."

"*Buster* gave her that impression, huh?" Calum smirked.

"Or she easily came to that conclusion on her own. I guess my dating history isn't much of a secret around this town," Harris admitted mostly to himself. Sure, he'd maybe enjoyed the singles scene in Spring Forest a bit more than most. Over the past year, though, he'd slowed down considerably to focus more on work. He'd rather grab a beer with buddies or put in some extra hours at one of his houses than go out on another date that always left him searching for something more. "But Elise is different. *I'm* different when we're together.

There's something about her that makes me want to protect her, but at the same time introduce her to everything she missed out on when she was living under her aunt's thumb."

"Speaking of Regina Mackenzie..." Lucy's eyes flashed with curiosity. "Any word from her?"

Harris shook his head. "I know Elise spoke with a detective the other day about the case, but it doesn't sound like there have been any updates. Something's fishy about the entire situation. I mean, besides the whole disappearance after embezzling money from a charity thing."

"That reminds me, I need to put together a basket for the silent auction Elise organized." Lucy grabbed another wing out of her container and carried it with her to a shelf with a discreet sign that simply said Animals.

"Did Elise hit you up for a donation too?" Harris asked Calum. Canvasing the local business owners to solicit donations was a big step for an introvert who was still emerging from her social cocoon.

"Yep. She stopped by Pins and Pints yesterday to pick up a gift card." Calum stepped closer to Harris and lowered his voice. "She left me half a dozen pecan pie bars that I was supposed to take home to Lucy. But I accidentally ate them all. So now I need to send in another gift card before she'll share the recipe with me."

"See what I mean about her changing into a

butterfly and getting things done?" Harris's chest pushed forward with pride, as though he was somehow responsible for Elise's boost in confidence and negotiation skills. "She's like a whole new person."

Calum, though, quickly brought him back down to reality. "Just don't expect her transformation to take place according to your schedule, man. You might be the best at making over houses, but you can't make over people."

Chapter Eight

"What time did you say the window installers were coming?" Elise asked Harris on Friday as he stood on a ladder in the dining room of the colonial on Dawson Avenue. He was rewiring the electrical box to recenter the antique chandelier and she was holding his ladder steady.

The man might grumble about some of the changes Elise wanted to make, but he always let her take the lead. Kind of like how he did a couple weeks ago when they were making out—

"They're not supposed to be here until next Thursday," he answered, yanking her thoughts back to the present. "Why?"

Elise cleared her throat, trying to pretend she wasn't still thinking about their kiss a couple of weeks later. "Because someone just pulled into the driveway with a truck and travel trailer."

Without missing a turn of his screwdriver, Harris asked, "Is it a blue truck with a white-and-gray trailer that says Adventure Awaits on the back?"

Elise bent at the waist so she could peek out the open front door without letting go of the ladder. "Maybe? I can't see the back from here. Were you expecting someone?"

"Not really. But my parents like to stop by unannounced every time they're leaving or returning to Asheville from one of their trips."

"They're *here*?" Elise's voice came out in a squeak and she backed away from the ladder, searching for the nearest exit route. "Your parents? Right now?"

Unfortunately for Harris, her panic had caused her to let go right as he was on his way down. By the time he got to the fourth rung, the aluminum frame began to wobble, and he lost his balance. Harris was able to jump free and plant both of his boots on the ground just as the ladder crashed into the wall, leaving a big gash in the fresh wallpaper sample Miguel had hung there an hour ago.

"Sorry," she murmured right as someone called out from the porch, "Knock, knock."

Ugh. She'd missed her opportunity to dart out

the back before Harris's parents could see her. As the older couple approached, though, Elise found that instead of her nerves twitching with anxiety as they normally would have, they were humming with anticipation. In fact, she was curious to know more about Harris Vega's family.

Still. She wished the rest of the crew hadn't already taken off early for one of the subcontractor's bachelor party weekend. It meant she couldn't blend into the normal chaos of the jobsite and observe things from a distance.

She hung back in the newly widened archway between the dining room and the entry as Harris met the older couple at the door. He hugged his mom first, then shook his dad's hand before pulling the man into a one-armed embrace.

"I thought you guys weren't driving home until next week…"

"Why aren't you wearing the new shirt I sent you from Key West…?"

"I see you went with the cedar for the front porch…"

All three of them began speaking at once, quickly pinballing between multiple conversations at the same time. Elise's eyes were riveted and her ears worked overtime as she listened to them discuss cutting their Florida trip short due to a hurricane, the impracticality of a white linen guayabera shirt on a construction site and whether redwood would have been a better choice for the outdoor steps.

Just when Elise thought she could slip away unnoticed, his mom looked right at her and said, "Are you hungry? You look hungry. Harris never bothers stopping to eat when he's working. We swung through the barbecue place on our way into town and picked up some pulled pork sandwiches. They're still hot. Speaking of hot, did you get that *Hadestown* playlist I sent you?"

"Mom, maybe we should do some introductions before you start passing out the food and launching into song?" Harris's grin was only somewhat apologetic. "Elise, this is my mom, Cindy Vega, whose missions in life are to feed people and to teach middle schoolers the lyrics to every musical on Broadway. Mom, this is Elise Mackenzie, who happens to be a phenomenal cook and actually packed some… um…" Harris looked at Elise. "What *did* you bring for today's lunch break?"

"I brought chicken salad sandwiches, but I think Buster snuck off with yours like a regular Jean Valjean slipping past Inspector Javert."

"*Les Mis* reference! I love it." Cindy nodded conspiratorially at Elise. "My son can be as relentless about his remodels as Javert and almost never takes time for a lunch break. Just like he insists his employees never work weekends, but then always stays behind and finishes every little project himself. Oh well. At least Buster was able to enjoy the sandwiches. That foreman needs to eat more."

Harris rolled his eyes. "Buster's doctor might disagree with you, Mom. She actually just told him he needs to lose twenty pounds."

"My doctor told me the same thing," Harris's father said. Cindy swatted her hand at the air dismissively. "But your mother here, thinks everyone is too skinny."

"Dad," Harris said to the man who had the same build and features as him, but with a few more wrinkles, pounds and a head of gray hair. "I'm not sure if you remember Elise, John Mackenzie's daughter. Elise, this is my dad, Simon Vega."

She reached out to shake his hand, which was warm and weathered, but still strong. "It's nice to meet you both, Mr. and Mrs. Vega."

"Oh, I remember you from way back when you were this big." Simon lowered his palm to measure a couple of feet from the ground. He had the faintest accent, slightly rolling his r's and occasionally using a hard i. "You used to follow your dad all around the dealership, quiet as a little mouse. But with the same curious eyes."

"That's right." Elise tried to smile, but something tugged at the edges of her heart. Whoa. Since this was her father's hometown, it wasn't exactly rare to run into people who remembered him, but it always moved her to share those memories. Elise had a deep-seated need to hear more. "Harris said you used to work at Mackenzie Motors. Did you know my dad very well?"

The older man's eyes softened at something in the distance, and her heart beat several times before he finally answered. "The day I met your father changed my life."

"I sense a narrative backstory. Our audience is going to need some sandwiches for this," Cindy announced before hurrying off to retrieve the food.

Simon followed his son, who led them to the "break room" which consisted of five mismatched chairs circled around a spool of rubber conduit in the front parlor. "My brother and I had just moved here from Mexico with a friend who'd gotten us jobs on a fishing boat out of Wanchese. The first trip out, though, I got so seasick, I swore I'd never get on another boat. But I also needed a job, otherwise, I couldn't stay here on my work visa. I tried to get hired at one of the nearby fisheries, but the smell reminded me of that first day on the boat and I couldn't make it through the interview before running to the bathroom to—"

"Lunch is served!" Cindy interrupted her husband just in time. As she passed out the food, she paused to stage-whisper to Elise. "It's best not to get him going when it comes to seafood. Simon couldn't even make it through the first act of *The Little Mermaid*. Thirty plus years of marriage and I haven't been able to bring home so much as a tuna fish sandwich."

The thought of canned tuna reminded Elise of Oliver and the first time she and Harris had fed the feral cats. She had no idea if Harris had caught the reference, but the memory, coupled with his knowing gaze was enough to send a tingle up the back of her neck.

Needing to get the attention off her, Elise asked Simon, "So then how did you meet my dad?"

"I was at a gas station in Rocky Mount, using my last five dollars to fill up the tank of the 1965 Scout my brother and I drove up from Mexico. This middle-aged white man in a fancy suit starts asking me questions about the car. I was still learning English at the time, so I knew I was messing up the answers. Then he switches to Spanish. And that only makes me more nervous. I'm thinking, why is this man asking so many questions and how did he get so fluent? Is he an immigration officer? Is he going to find out about my work visa and have me sent back?"

"Oh wow." Elise had experienced moments of feeling as though she didn't belong somewhere, but she'd never had to live in fear of being deported. "That must have been very scary for you."

Simon nodded and his wife leaned toward him, putting a hand on his arm, and giving him a reassuring squeeze before he continued. "Anyway, this man keeps talking and finally asks if I want to sell the car. Obviously, I can't sell it without talking to my brother first since it's the only thing we own. But Julio's gone on the boat and won't be back for a few days. I'm curious, so I ask the man how much he'd pay. He says five thousand dollars. I almost handed him the keys right there. It was a lot of money back then and I still hadn't found a job. But I tell him that I can't sell it until my brother gets back. He hands me his business card with a phone number so I can call him after I talk to Julio. I see the name of the business is the same as his last name. So I think he must be the owner and maybe he'll give me a job. I didn't even know where Spring Forest was—or that it was two hours away—but I asked him if he had any work for me. He says, 'Do you like cars?' Just like that. And I think to myself, I like that they take me where I need to go. I liked to watch *Miami Vice* and they drove a Ferrari so I liked *that* car. I say sure, but really, I didn't know the first thing about them except they needed gas and gas costs money, which meant I needed a job. John tells me to follow him to his car dealership so I can see where I'd be working if he hires me. Then he holds up his keys and says, 'But it's been a long time since I've driven one of these. Would you mind driving my car?'"

"That sounds exactly like something my dad would say. And who could blame him for wanting to get behind the wheel of a '65 Scout? Especially since that was the year the eight hundreds came out."

Simon lifted his eyes at his son. "The lady knows her cars."

Harris's grin was wide as he winked at Elise. "She really does."

Great, now his parents were going to see her blush. She cleared her throat. "So, you drove my dad's car all the way to Spring Forest?"

"Yes. It was a brand new Porsche 911 Turbo. It might as well have been the Ferrari from *Miami Vice*, because I was sweating the entire time it took me to drive it here. But John never complained that I went so slow and couldn't keep up with him. I thought for sure he was going to figure out that I didn't know the first thing about cars since I was terrified to take it out of fourth gear. Instead, he says that he appreciated the fact that I was so respectful with the Porsche. I could've raced it and revved the engine, but I took good care of someone else's property. He told me I could start the next day. At first, I did the basic stuff, like sweeping the showroom and running for parts. Then, as I got used to how things worked and got more confident, John asked me if I wanted to be promoted to a salesperson. But I liked being around the cars more than around the people. So he had me train with the mechanics and I loved it."

"Did you always work at the Spring Forest dealership?" Elise asked. She'd visited the original location with her dad whenever they came to town, but it had been so long ago.

"Yes. When John opened the second place in Raleigh, he decided to make that the headquarters. I went with him for a couple of weeks to hire and train the new mechanics and he wanted me to stay on there as the service manager. But by then I'd already married Cindy and we'd had Oscar and were settled in Spring Forest."

Elise tilted her head at the mention of another family member. Harris realized he'd only mentioned his brother in passing before. "Oscar is my older brother. He took over Dad's shop when my parents retired and moved to Asheville. He's the one who inherited the Vega skill with engines."

"But you're skilled with refurbishing houses," Cindy pointed out, as any proud mom would. Then she told Elise, "Ever since he was a little boy, Harris could build the most creative things. First it was birdhouses—I think we had an entire flock of pigeons living in our backyard one summer. Then he moved on to doghouses and the most intricate cat condos. He always loved taking care of animals."

Elise had seen for herself his fondness for dogs and, well, the *non*-feral cats. Her boss at Barkyard Boarding had told her that Harris usually donated his building skills to Furever Paws when they were in need of extra pens outside or an addition to the dog play area.

The subject soon turned to his parents' recent trip to Florida and then to Harris's brother, Oscar. Elise finished her sandwich as she listened to the family chat about family things. They tried to include her in the conversation, but she was happy to just be an observer. Especially since the pace of the conversation went so quickly, the topics jumped from one thing to the next as they caught up with each other.

Her turn to talk, though, happened sooner than she'd expected. Harris stood up to offer his parents a tour of the house and the work in progress. Yet he deferred most of the couple's questions to Elise.

"Are you going to keep the master bedroom closet on this side?" Cindy asked at one point.

"No," Harris replied, and Elise held her breath because she knew he'd been reluctant about replacing a load-bearing wall with several open beams. Then he nudged her and said, "Lise, tell them your suggestion for the en suite dressing area."

So she did.

"What kind of tile are you guys putting in this hallway bathroom?" Simon wanted to know a few moments later.

"Counters, vanities, and flooring are all Elise," Harris explained before asking her, "Do you want me to go grab the samples from the truck?"

The tour and questions went on for almost an

hour and each time Elise explained an idea, Harris beamed at her like a spotlight from across the room. His pride and confidence in her and her opinions was infectious and by the time they ended up in the kitchen, Elise was easily responding without any prompting at all. In fact, she was pretty sure Harris had left them at one point to go finish the rewiring for the chandelier and she'd barely even noticed.

After Simon had convinced them to retrofit the garage and Cindy had asked for Elise's pumpkin fudge recipe—they'd paused for a dessert break after climbing to the third-floor cupola—Elise and Harris walked his parents out to their truck to say their goodbyes.

"Hey, Elise," Simon said right before he climbed into the cab. "If you don't mind me asking, whatever happened to you father's collection of cars? He had quite a few, including the Scout that he eventually talked me and my brother into selling him."

Harris held his breath, hoping the unexpected question didn't cause Elise to retreat into that wall of privacy she usually kept between herself and everyone else around her. After the initial awkwardness of his parents' surprise visit—his ankle was still throbbing due to his unfortunate dismount from the ladder when she'd suddenly let go of it—she'd seemed so relaxed and even talkative as she'd led the tour of the house.

However, he'd already learned that discussing furniture placement and discussing her family were two completely different things. Just when Harris thought he was going to have to change the subject, Elise finally sighed.

"I used to go to the auto auctions with my father and one time we saw a yellow Scout 800. Dad told me that he had one just like it in his offsite warehouse that he was holding on to for a friend."

Harris didn't often see his dad shed a tear, but there was definitely a dampness in Simon Vega's eyes. The older man rubbed his chin thoughtfully. "When the boys were little and Cindy went back to school to get her teaching certification, we didn't want to take out a loan. John insisted on paying me top dollar to buy the car and promised that I could drive it whenever I wanted. But we were always so busy with work and Cindy's rehearsals and the kids' sports. Then I opened my own shop and I guess we just lost track of time. I should have tried harder to stay in touch with him."

"It's better that you remember how he was before the Alzheimer's finally took hold of him. At least that's what I try and tell myself." Elise's lips quivered slightly, but she still managed a smile at Simon. Harris couldn't imagine how painful it would be to slowly lose his own father to a disease like that. She was so strong to be able to talk about her experience. "Most people don't know this, but my dad was pretty deep in debt by the time he went into the assisted living facility. My aunt had to sell most of the cars to help pay off his creditors—and even that wasn't enough to cover all the costs of his care. The only car I put up a fight to keep was the minivan he'd bought my mom when they'd first got married. Regina knew that she couldn't get much money for it, so it stayed behind when the auction guys came."

Harris couldn't stop himself from putting his hand on Elise's shoulder, trying to offer her some comfort, or at least remind her that while her family was gone, she wasn't totally alone. Her muscles immediately eased under his palm and he took it as a reassuring sign that she relaxed rather than shied away from him.

"That doesn't make sense." Harris's drama-loving mom was the first to voice the same concern he himself had politely avoided. "Simon, didn't you tell me that John Mackenzie was one of the most astute businessmen you'd ever met?"

His dad nodded. "When he sold all the dealerships, he made a fortune. It's hard to imagine anyone losing that much money, but it's even harder to think someone as smart as John let his finances get that bad."

Elise's shoulders rose and fell under Harris's arm as she shrugged. "All I know is that my dad sold the dealership right after my mom was diagnosed so he could spend more time at home with the two of us. His mind started slipping a couple of years after that. My aunt told me that's when he made quite a few bad investments."

Harris could see the doubt in both of his parents' faces. Elise must have also noticed it because she started avoiding eye contact, sneaking glances in the direction of the house and then toward her car. She was looking for an exit route, a quick escape from the turn in the conversation.

"I…uh…didn't realize how late it's getting, and I need to stop by Furever Paws and drop off some silent auction baskets before I head home."

Harris wasn't sure how many donations she'd been able to secure for the animal shelter's fund-raiser, but from the little banners hanging in shop windows that he'd seen all over town, it looked like most of the businesses he frequented had already contributed something. He had no doubt that she would be eager to turn over anything she received directly to Bethany or the Whitaker sisters. Elise didn't have to say it, but Harris knew that she didn't want anyone thinking she was like her aunt and might abscond with something that didn't belong to her.

"I was about to close up here too," he said. "Maybe I'll follow you out to the shelter to check and see if the lumber company delivered the wood and scaffolding poles we need to start framing the runway."

"What runway?" his mom wanted to know. "What are Bunny and Birdie building now? Can it double as a stage? I've always thought they have a great location for a small outdoor amphitheater."

"Are you using cedar for that too?" his dad asked, because the man had strong opinions about building materials.

"Elise is in charge of the Furever Paws fundraiser," Harris explained. "And we're probably just going with plywood because it's a temporary structure for the doggy beauty pageant she's hosting."

"Oh, I'm not *hosting* it," Elise corrected, her eyes wide and both palms raised in a stopping motion. "I'm just helping with the organizing. Also, technically, it's a fashion show. Plus a silent auction. And a cutest pet contest. But they're all separate events."

"I wish *you'd* get a pet, Harris," his mom said out of absolutely nowhere. "If you're not going to give me grandbabies anytime soon, then you might as well get some practice looking after something besides that wilted plant in your office."

"Mom, you're always telling me I can barely feed myself." Harris fought the urge to ease the tension forming at the bridge of his nose. "Where am I going to find the time to take care of an animal?"

"Elise will help you," his mom offered on behalf

of the young woman beside him who was biting her lower lip, either due to mortification or to keep herself from laughing. Probably the latter. "You said she helps feed all those wild cats behind the Maple Street house and she's been feeding you and your entire crew lately."

"Which means Elise is busy enough as it is. And so am I. Why don't you and Dad get a pet?" Harris crossed his arms defensively. "Captain Whiskers died over a year ago."

"I've been telling your mother the same thing. Our neighbor has a bearded dragon that likes to come over to our place and visit." His dad turned to Elise. "Could we enter *him* in the cutest pet contest?"

"Sure, but Igor would probably lose," Harris muttered under his breath. Mrs. Castellano's overgrown lizard liked to escape its habitat and sun itself on his parents' front patio. Harris had nearly jumped out of his boots the last time he'd been in Asheville for a visit.

Elise used her elbow to nudge him. "Actually, there's been enough interest that we opened a Coolest Reptile category. Let me get you a flyer from my car."

Rolling his eyes, Harris walked away to lock up the house while she promised to send his parents pictures of the animals available for adoption...by someone other than him. The Adventure

Awaits trailer was already gone and Elise was in her minivan—which Harris was viewing in a different light, now that he knew it held sentimental value to her—when he returned to the driveway.

"Hey, since we're going to the same place, why don't I just hop in and ride with you?" Harris opened the passenger door and climbed inside before she could come up with an excuse. "Then maybe we can stop somewhere in town on the way back and grab a bite to eat."

"How can you even think of food after those humongous barbecue sandwiches your parents brought us? Between those and all the baking I've been doing lately, I'm going to need to buy bigger pants."

He let his eyes scan down the length of her jeans. "I think you fill those ones out rather well."

A pink flush crept up her neck and he bit back a smug smile.

"Your mom and dad are very nice," Elise said before pulling out of the driveway so quickly, she fishtailed the back tires in the loose gravel.

"Are you hoping that by changing the subject to my parents, I won't want to talk about how good you look in your jeans? Or how I can't stop thinking about how soft your hair felt when it was spread out on the wet floor beneath—" Harris stopped speaking so he could focus on not getting thrown from his seat as Elise took a sharp turn. "I'm not exactly a slow driver myself, but do you *always* go this fast?"

"Only when I'm in a hurry to get someplace. Or to get you to stop talking."

Harris chanced a quick glance into the back seat. "Well, you can either talk to me about that kiss we shared the other night, or you can risk having the rest of the silent auction baskets topple over before we deliver them. But you can't do both."

Elise lifted her foot from the accelerator, but only slightly. "Why can't we talk about anything besides that?"

"Because I liked it. And I think you liked it too. In fact, since we both enjoyed it so much, we should probably be doing it more often."

"I don't think that would be such a good idea," she said, picking up the speed as they merged onto the highway. There were fewer turns now, so she could go as fast as she wanted without messing up the perfectly arranged baskets.

"Why not?"

"Because you're my boss and my landlord."

"Okay, that's true. But I'm also your friend."

She turned her face enough to give him a side-eye. "Do you make out with all of your friends, who also happen to be your employees and tenants?"

"Not Buster. At least not anymore."

He could've sworn he heard a smothered chuckle.

"How about this?" Harris's fingers tightened on the armrest as they approached the turnoff to Little Creek Road. Was this how people felt in his truck when he was going well over the posted speed limit? "I want to respect your boundaries, so I won't try and kiss you again. But if *you* decide that you want to kiss me, I'll be ready and available. Again."

"Is this your way of trying to shift the power balance to me to make it seem like a more level playing field? Or is this your way of preemptively blaming me in case something goes wrong, which it most likely will?"

"That's a negative attitude." Harris made a *tsking* sound. "Especially considering the fact that, technically, you were the one who kissed me first that night."

"Well, what did you expect me to do when you positioned your lips so close to me like that?"

"Is that all it took?" Harris smiled and Elise groaned, probably knowing she'd admitted more than she'd intended. "I'll be sure to keep my mouth in close proximity if it'll help."

Elise pulled into a space, put the car in Park, then turned to face him. "Has anyone ever said no to you, Harris Vega?"

"Besides Buster? And my mom? And you? No."

Chapter Nine

Harris carried in the last of the donations from Elise's car and found her talking with Bethany Robeson near the reception desk. After passing the cellophane-covered gift basket to another volunteer, he pulled an envelope out of his back pocket.

"I found this on the floorboard." He had no doubt that the thing had toppled out when Elise had made that sharp right turn off Dawson Avenue. "I'm not sure which basket it goes in, though."

"Thanks." Elise took the envelope from him. "This is the gift certificate for four rounds of golf at that new course in Kingdom Creek. I was thinking it would fetch a pretty good price all on its own."

"It will." Harris made a mental note to place a bid for himself. "I've been there once—Ian Parsons was able to get us a tee time since he lives in the community. The fairways are absolutely incredible, but between both of our crazy schedules, we were only able to make it through nine holes. We owe each other a rematch."

"In that case, I'll be sure to steer you both toward the auction table in the hopes of a little bidding war." Elise quickly dashed Harris's hopes for a sure win before turning her attention back to the director of Furever Paws. "Ian and Rachel said they'll be bringing the twins to the event next week. They registered Pepper for the fashion show but didn't think their cat Salty would be willing to walk the runway."

"Speaking of cats," Bethany said. "The wire transfer from Feline Finest came in today. One of their vice presidents is planning to attend the fundraiser and asked if we could arrange a photo op of them handing us an oversized cardboard check."

"I think we can work that into the ceremony, maybe right before the silent auction goes live so that it'll encourage other donors to be just as generous." Elise might be shy, but she definitely knew how to fundraise. "Oh, and did you see the email I forwarded you from that start-up company outside of Greensboro that specializes in fashionable collars and leashes? They can't afford the corporate sponsorship but asked if we'd be willing to do a collaboration on social media. They're sending you a free box of some of their best-selling products to try out before we commit."

"Around here, we can certainly use all the free collars and leashes we can get." Bethany clasped her hands together. "I can't believe you've put all this together in such a short amount of time."

Elise ducked her head and half shrugged, but she couldn't hide the proud smile Harris was becoming accustomed to seeing. "It's the least I could do."

"The least?" Bunny Whitaker came walking into the reception area. "Between the online entry fees for that cutest pet contest and the corporate sponsorships, you've already more than made up the money from before. And that's not including the donations we usually bring in at our events or the money we expect to make off the silent auction."

Harris's rib cage felt as though it would burst with pride, even though all he'd contributed to the fundraiser so far was the offer to build the runway stage. But like he'd told Lucy and Calum back at the bookshop, watching Elise bloom like this before his very eyes was its own reward.

Birdie Whitaker, Bunny's older no-nonsense sister, appeared just then holding a golden ball of fluff in her arms. "Harris, you're just the man I wanted to see. A big rig is out back unloading a bunch of crates with your name on them."

"That should be the scaffolding and plywood I ordered," he told the older woman.

"Here, take Pancake for me," Birdie said before passing off her furry bundle to Elise. A little puppy head lifted only slightly, revealing huge brown eyes, before snuggling back to sleep in Elise's arms. "Harris, you come with me so we can get that truck out of the way before Stew gets here."

"Why would my boyfriend care about a bunch of wood and crates?" Bunny adjusted one of the straps on her denim overalls.

"I'm sure he wouldn't," her sister responded. "But the big rig is parked right where Stew parks. If we don't get it moved, your boyfriend is going to plant that ginormous RV of his in front of our house permanently."

"Would that be such a terrible thing?" The two sisters didn't bother to lower their voices as they walked through the front door. "I like having Stew around and you're usually spending the nights over at Doc J's anyway…"

"Is this Buttercup's last unadopted puppy?" Harris asked before he had to hear the rest of the older ladies' conversation. He scratched between the tiny pup's ears. "I heard she had a heart murmur."

"That's what the vet says," Bethany sighed. "It's still too early to determine how serious it is, though. She gets another ultrasound in a couple of weeks and we'll have a better idea of how to proceed."

Elise looked up from where she was nestling her face against the puppy's neck. Her cheek was inches away from Harris's hand. "You mean Pancake's still not eligible for adoption?"

"Not yet, unfortunately. We need her spayed before we can place her, and she can't have any sort of surgery until we get the okay from the cardiac specialist."

The glass front door opened, and Birdie impatiently called out, "Harris, are you coming or not?"

It was all he could do to pull himself away from Elise and Pancake and the charming picture they made together. As he walked outside, he wondered if ordering Elise the book on plumbing had been the wrong gift idea. Maybe what he really wanted to get her was a pet of her own.

Luckily, Harris had been so preoccupied with the delivery of the runway materials that Elise found him a ride back into town with Wendy Alvarez, a Furever Paws volunteer who coordinated with the Pets for Vets charity and who also happened to rent one of Harris's properties.

Maybe Elise should've said goodbye to Harris before she'd driven off, but it was already emotional enough hearing that heart-tugging story about her father from Mr. Vega and then tearing herself away from the shy, yet snuggly Pancake. The last thing she wanted to add to her overwhelming day was another conversation about that kiss they'd shared.

"Are you sure you don't mind giving him a lift?" Elise had asked Wendy, who'd stopped by the shelter with her boyfriend's working dog, Jedi. Wendy trained dogs as emotional support animals for veterans with PTSD, but the woman was also very astute when it came to humans. A few months ago, when Wendy had dropped off a donation check with Regina, Elise had found herself telling the woman all about her father and her life history.

"It's no problem," Wendy assured her. "In fact, I should probably talk to him anyway. I'm moving in with Greg and need to give Harris a thirty-day notice."

First Bethany, then Josie and now Wendy. It seemed like all the single women Elise knew were falling in love. As happy as she was for them, it was difficult not to feel as though she was behind the relationship curve compared to everyone else.

"It's always been like that, though," she told Mr. Frankfurter after the dachshund scratched at the kitchen door on Sunday afternoon to watch her do her usual prepping and cooking for the upcoming week. "I guess I'm what you might call a late bloomer."

But the dog wasn't listening. He was waddling toward the front door, getting ready to bark just as a knock sounded. It was Roxy from across the street with the halter and leash in her hand. "Sorry he snuck over here again. Brandon and I took him for a walk to the park and we...uh...got a little distracted."

The blush on Roxy's cheeks and the guilty way the teenage boy beside her intently studied the sky instead of making eye contact suggested that the young couple hadn't exactly been distracted by talk of homecoming dance outfits this time. However, Mr. Frankfurter had clearly forgiven his owner—or else he was just bored with hearing Elise talk about her lack of a social life—and happily allowed Roxy to slip on his halter and lead him home.

Returning to the kitchen, a weight settled over Elise with every passing minute of silence. She'd always thought she preferred being alone, but now her house suddenly felt...well...lonely.

Sure, she still appreciated the quiet, especially after a day filled with either barking or buzz saws. But these past few weeks she'd gradually grown accustomed to being around so many animals and people when she was at work or on the jobsite. It now felt odd when she was on her own.

She switched on the radio and tightened her apron, determined to keep herself too busy to feel anything. Unfortunately, before her big pot of chili had even reached a simmer, she was thinking about calling Harris and inviting him over for dinner.

But how did one even do that?

By the time she put the corn bread in the oven, she'd convinced herself to go visit Pancake, the timid puppy over at the shelter, instead. No, that could be a bad idea. She wouldn't want to get too attached. Maybe she should go to the coffee shop with her laptop and work from there. No, she'd already blown most of this week's food budget at the grocery store and the coffee shop wouldn't let her sit there unless she bought something. Besides, her nerves were jittery enough as it was. The last thing she needed right now was more caffeine.

Another knock sounded at the front door and instead of experiencing the usual instinct to ignore it, Elise was eager for the distraction of possibly having a visitor.

Instead, it was Roxy again and she was holding a stack of mail.

"I forgot to bring this over earlier. My mom said the post office sent it to our house by mistake." A much newer minivan than Elise's honked from across the street and Mrs. Cole waved at them. "We gotta go to my grandma's for Sunday dinner. Her brownies taste like cardboard compared to yours and her Wi-Fi reception sucks. But my mom says we have to make time for family responsibilities. Plus, Grandma says I can try on some of her jewelry to see if she has anything that'll work with my homecoming dress. Anyway, here."

Elise looked at the stack thrust into her hands.

The twenty or so envelopes and postcards with yellow forwarding labels were a wake-up call, reminding her of her past address and her past life. She had no desire to deal with any of that tonight.

The timer dinged and Elise set down the mail to turn off the oven. She quickly forgot about sorting through the envelopes because her phone alarm beeped telling her it was time to feed the cats. Next came all the other adult tasks she could think of to stay busy and prove herself an independent adult. Like laundry, research on the best table for the formal dining room at the Dawson Avenue property, dinner, research on wood shutters for the Maple Street house and then checking the cutest pet contest website to see how many views and votes they'd gotten. Holy cow. A million views already? She scrolled through the pictures, somewhat surprised that the Coolest Reptile posts were getting the most votes.

Elise fell asleep with her old laptop open on the bed beside her and woke up the next morning to a text from Harris asking if she was available after work today to go with him to The Lighting District, a discount warehouse store, to pick out some light fixtures. Since it was right next door to Stone and Slab, where Elise had planned to go anyway to get a quote on the granite for the kitchen island, she replied with a thumbs-up emoji.

If he'd been annoyed about her ditching him at

the animal shelter on Friday, he thankfully didn't seem to be holding it against her. Elise grabbed a sweater from her closet because it might be chilly when she got off work. Not because it was the burnt orange V-neck that Roxy saw her wearing last week and said, "Look at you, Miss Elise. You're killing it in that top today."

Spying the stack of mail she'd forgotten on the table last night, Elise scooped it up, along with her stainless steel travel mug full of coffee, and didn't give it a second thought until her lunch break.

She was more than halfway through the pile of what was mostly junk mail when Lucy Tucker and Calum Ramsey came in the door with a very sweet but nervous Buttercup. The couple also seemed rather apprehensive, like most of the new pet parents who were boarding their precious fur babies for the first time.

"Hey, Buttercup," Elise spoke directly to the dog. Even though she'd been in contact with the bookshop and bowling alley owners for fundraiser donations, sometimes it was still easier to direct her attention to animals. "I saw one of your pups on Friday. She let me hold her for a while. In fact, I saved the shirt I was wearing that day because I knew you were coming in and I thought it might help you adjust to have a familiar scent during your first stay with us."

Elise pulled the flannel button-up from the tote

bag underneath the reception desk. Lucy chuckled then retrieved a few items from her own bag.
"Great minds must think alike because I brought
along Calum's pillowcase and her favorite stuffed
animal from the store."

Calum jerked his head at his fiancée. "Why *my*
pillowcase?"

"Because Buttercup loves curling up on your
side of the bed. Anyway, it's not like you'll be
using it while we're gone." Lucy turned back to
Elise and patted her round belly. "We're going on
a last-minute babymoon before we become full-
time parents."

Buttercup tilted her blond head at Calum, who
corrected, "Full-time *human* parents."

Elise smiled with the couple, but as she got Buttercup settled in one of the mini rooms with her bed
and food dishes, she couldn't stop wondering what
it would be like to have a romantic getaway with a
significant other. Heck, she wouldn't even mind a
getaway all by herself. A little trip where she could
leave town for a few days and forget about the ru-
mors surrounding her aunt and all the extra work
and volunteer duties Elise had taken on. But that
afternoon, every time she imagined herself sunbath-
ing on a tropical beach or sitting before a roaring
fire at a luxury ski resort somewhere, Harris would
always pop into her daydream uninvited.

Elise had just changed out of her work shirt and

was collecting her stuff at the end of her shift when she saw the remaining half of the forwarded mail left to sort. She decided she might as well get this over with.

Letter asking if she was ready to upgrade her heating and air conditioning-unit, toss.

Postcard reminder for her next dental exam, keep.

Financial aid packet from the University of Spring Forest listing scholarships and application deadlines for the upcoming semester. Toss. No, keep. She'd always planned to go to college eventually, maybe she could take some online classes once the pet fashion show was over. It'd be way easier now that she didn't have her aunt complaining that Elise didn't have the time.

When she saw the final piece of mail, her knees went weak. And not in a good way. She landed in the desk chair with a thud as she stared at the return address. "Eternal Memories—Celebrations of Life."

The red PAST DUE stamp was right below Elise's name.

"Is Princess's dad late again?" Shane set his clipboard on the reception desk, startling Elise. "Everyone else has been picked up from doggy day care."

She quickly hugged the letter close to her chest, not wanting her boss to see the unexpected delinquent notice. "Uh…he called twenty minutes ago and said he'd be here by five thirty."

"You okay?" Shane asked. "You look all pale and tense."

"Just tired." Elise willed some color back into her cheeks while crinkling the envelope tighter in her hand.

"I hear you've been burning the candle at both ends, Elise. Bethany said you've turned the whole fundraiser around, all while working two jobs." Shane turned his head as Harris swung open one of the wide glass doors. "Speaking of which, it looks like your other employer is here to collect you for your next shift."

Elise quickly stood, for once relieved that the blush she got whenever Harris was around might mask the fact that less than two minutes ago the blood had completely drained from her face. "What are you doing here?"

"I thought we had a date." Harris flashed that charming smile of his, practically daring Elise to correct him in front of Shane before continuing. "To go to The Lighting District. Or did you plan to have Wendy drop me off there to meet you, as well?"

Okay, so maybe he *had* been a little annoyed that Elise had ditched him on Friday afternoon. But it wasn't like she'd left him stranded. His smile slipped when his eyes dropped to the letter she was still clutching.

Before he could ask about it, though, she shoved

it under her keep pile next to her tote bag. "Sorry. I need to stay until Princess gets picked up."

"Go ahead and take off," Shane offered. "I'll cover the front desk. I'm not meeting Bethany at Veniero's until later. She finally talked the Whitaker sisters into getting a new coffee maker and the delivery person hasn't dropped it off yet. She wants to get it out of the box and set up before they see how fancy it is and send it back."

"Thank God. I was there this morning showing my crew where the stage was going to be set up and Bunny offered us a cup of something that looked like coffee but tasted like campfire ash. Anyway, we should probably get going before the warehouse closes." Harris's eyes dropped to Elise's tote bag, sitting there by the mail and her empty travel mug. "Want me to give you a hand carrying your stuff?"

"I've got it. See you tomorrow, Shane." She grabbed everything so quickly to head out the front door that her awkward grip resulted in the mail slipping from her fingers by the time she made it to the parking lot.

"We should probably take my truck…" Harris spoke right as everything fell from Elise's hand.

She couldn't do anything but watch the letter flutter downward in slow motion until it landed on the gravel, the red PAST DUE stamp practically flashing between them. Harris knelt to pick up the papers and her tote bag, which had spilled even more of her personal belongings onto the asphalt—like her sports bra that she'd changed out of after jogging with some of the faster dogs today.

The mortification almost paralyzed her. Almost. Springing into action, she dropped to her knees and shoved everything into the bag. Except she was too flustered and too rushed and the one thing she hadn't wanted him to see toppled right back out.

Harris picked it up and turned it over in his hands. "Is this from when your father passed away?"

"I'm not sure. I just got it and haven't opened it yet."

"Don't you think you should?"

Elise saw Princess's dad pull into the parking lot and her throat constricted several times before she forced out a response. "Not here."

She opened the passenger side door of Harris's truck and climbed in. Not because she wanted to ride with him, but because she knew the dam inside of her was about to bust open and she didn't want anyone else witnessing the tears she couldn't hold back.

Harris put her tote bag in the back seat and then got in on the driver's side, commanding himself to be patient. But it took every ounce of willpower he had not to pull her across the cab of the truck and hug her.

He gently set the letter on the console between them, as though it was a hot electrical fuse that might blow out the entire breaker box at any moment. But Elise didn't make a move to take it. Instead, she took several deep breaths while Harris sat there, watching her and wondering how he could fix something when he had no clue what was wrong.

"Do you want *me* to open it?" he finally asked.

Elise sighed. "No. I appreciate you trying to protect me, but this is something I'm going to have to face."

Her fingers trembled slightly as she tore open the envelope, her jaw tightening as she scanned the page before her. Then she blinked several times before looking away. Just when he was about to take the paper from her hands and read it himself, Elise finally said, "I don't get it. My father's funeral was five years ago. Aunt Regina made all the arrangements. How can they be sending me a bill now?"

"Didn't your aunt pay this Eternal Memories place?" He already knew the answer, though. He had a feeling they both did.

"I assumed she did. She always took care of the finances." Elise shook her head. "I remember going with her to make the final arrangements. It wasn't a traditional mortuary. It was more of an event venue with professional party planners, except instead of planning weddings, they planned funerals. Or celebrations of life, I guess. I tried to tell her that my father would have wanted a small service. He liked nice cars, but other than that, he wasn't a flashy man. But Regina insisted on putting on this big production. She said it would reflect badly on our family if she went cheap with his funeral. Since she was paying for it anyway, I decided not to argue so I left to go sit in the car. I wasn't even there when she ordered all this stuff." Elise showed him the invoice, pointing to one of the itemized lines. "Five thousand dollars for a gospel choir? Twenty thousand for the glass-enclosed horse-drawn carriage? I never had anything to do with picking any of this—or agreeing to be financially responsible for it. I certainly never signed anything. Why is my name listed as the customer in default?"

Harris's gut clenched, the way it always did when he heard about Elise's aunt, yet this time there was an added throbbing of rage. This wasn't the first time he'd heard of Regina Mackenzie skipping out on a bill, but it nearly made him sick to his stomach to think that she'd left her niece on the hook for this much money.

His first instinct was to write a check himself, but there was no way Elise would let him. Her newfound independence was too important to her. This was a woman who'd stayed up late three nights a week cooking for him and his whole crew because she didn't want to accept a free loan for staging furniture he wasn't even using. But he couldn't just sit here and do nothing.

His second instinct was to call his attorney. However, he couldn't do that unless Elise gave him the green light to share such a personal problem with a third party.

He needed to keep her talking until they could find a solution together. "I don't suppose there were any life insurance policies designated for funeral costs?"

Elise shrugged. "I have no idea. My aunt handled all of those things. I never questioned anything. I just… She said she was looking out for me, and I believed her. For years and years, it never even occurred to me to doubt her or question her. It took her stealing from the animal shelter and running out on all of us for my eyes to finally open. I can't believe how foolish I was."

"Lise." Harris lifted her chin forcing her eyes to meet his. The tears spiking her dark lashes were almost his undoing. "You were a kid when you moved in with her. A *sheltered* kid at that, moving in with family who you thought you could trust. How could you have possibly known otherwise? You should've seen some of the bad decisions I made when I was eighteen. And that was with both my parents and a big brother looking out for me. Don't be so hard on yourself. You'll handle this, just like you're handling the feral cat colony and the broken pipes and the pet fashion show and all of these other curve-balls coming at you."

Elise nodded, but she didn't look exactly convinced. He used his thumb to wipe away the dampness near her eye then asked, "Where's your little notepad where you make all those lists? You always seem to do your best thinking when you're writing out the next steps."

She sniffed. "I thought you hated my lists."

"I do when it's all the extra work you want me to do on the jobsite. Or the things that will end up costing me more money. But afterward, I'm always grateful for those lists because they keep us on schedule and will likely make us a bigger profit in the long run. Just pretend like this is another jobsite. What's first?"

"Maybe I should call the funeral place and see if I can negotiate the final amount due—or discuss some kind of payment schedule over time." She sat up straighter. "If they haven't been paid in five years, they might agree to settle for gradual payments since that would be better than nothing."

"That's my girl."

"Do you mind if I call now? Having you next to me makes me feel tougher, like I have backup."

Warmth spread through Harris's chest. "I'm always here for backup."

Elise dialed the number and was transferred from one person to the next as Harris studied the invoice.

His eye landed on a small detail just as Elise was leaving a message requesting a return call.

Harris glanced at the clock on his dash. "They've probably all gone home for the day. But check out the back page. There's a small column on the right with a payment history. It looks like twenty thousand was already paid by a wire transfer right after the funeral."

"That's not my aunt's bank, or at least not the one on the monthly statements that came in our mail." Elise studied the invoice, then she typed the name written in the payment line into her phone. "It's an investment firm based in New York. Who would've authorized that?"

"Maybe there was an insurance policy after all. Do you have any of your dad's old financial statements? Or a copy of his will that might give us some clues?"

Elise squeezed her eyes shut as she sagged against the seat. "I was in such a hurry to move out of my aunt's that I didn't even think to take my dad's death certificate with me, let alone important documents like that. Regina kept all that stuff in her study and the door was always locked when she wasn't in there anyway."

"Weren't you at the jobsite the other day when Buster lost the keys to the garage?" Harris asked, jerking his thumb toward his toolbox in the back of the pickup. "If I can't pick the lock, then I'll just take the door off the hinges."

"Right now?" Elise grabbed his hand—the one he'd used to wipe away her tears a few moments ago—and he could feel the anticipation spread from her palm into his skin. "But what about The Lighting District?"

Harris started the engine. "Looks like we'll have to move that date to tomorrow night."

Chapter Ten

"I knew I should've bought an extra bag of pickle-flavored sunflower seeds at the gas station this morning," Harris said casually as they drove past Pins and Pints, where three gourmet food trucks parked out front were already drawing lines of customers. "I'm pretty hungry and I try not to pick locks on an empty stomach. It breaks my concentration."

Elise handed him the homemade granola bar she'd packed in her tote bag this morning before skipping breakfast. "Eat this to tide you over. I'll buy you a bacon cheeseburger when we're done."

Luckily, Elise had remembered to run back to her

van and grab the garage door remote before they'd driven away from the Barkyard Boarding parking lot. It was one thing to pick a lock inside a house after you'd entered. It was a whole other thing to start with breaking and entering.

"As far as your aunt knows, you still live here, right?" Harris asked as he pulled his truck inside the garage.

"Yes. Although I told the detective that I moved out."

"In that case…" Harris quickly shut off the engine and pressed the button on the remote. "I'm glad we didn't go in through the front. I'd prefer not to attract any unwanted attention."

Elise's stomach dropped and she turned to him. "I don't want to put you in a bad position. If a patrol officer sees the lights on and gets suspicious, they might not treat you as fairly as they would me." She didn't want to think that the local police would show that kind of prejudice, but she couldn't ignore the possibility.

"Trust me, I've thought of that," Harris said, acknowledging the difference between their skin tones. "But two years ago, I remodeled the locker rooms at the station downtown. I talked the chief into building a custom weight room for the officers. All the cops in Spring Forest know me already. I'm more concerned with this being a possible crime scene and someone thinking we tampered with any evidence."

Elise gulped at the thought that her aunt could potentially be in a lot of trouble. Maybe it would be smarter to keep their distance. But before she could change her mind, Harris had already gotten out of the truck and was opening the mudroom door that led to the kitchen. She caught up in time to switch on the overhead light and saw everything looked exactly as she'd left it, minus the added layers of dust. The credit card she'd left behind was still on the kitchen counter, untouched. Nobody had been here since she'd left. That meant the investigation wasn't of such importance the detectives had executed a search warrant or put a seal on the place to secure evidence. At least not yet.

Still.

Her stomach was nauseated at the thought of sneaking into her aunt's study, a place she'd been expressly forbidden from entering when her aunt wasn't there to supervise. As she led Harris down the hall, she grew even more queasy at the thought of what she might find inside.

Elise stopped so abruptly, Harris ran into her back. "You don't think my aunt could possibly be… uh…you know…*in* her study?"

"Like not alive?" Harris asked rather casually as he knelt at the door. "Nah. I'm a contractor and would've recognized the smell if there was a body here."

Okay. That was good. She was angry with Regina, but she didn't want the woman dead.

"Maybe we should've brought gloves," she whispered as he slowly inserted a long wire into the keyhole.

"First of all, you probably don't need to whisper since nobody's home." The lock made a clicking sound and Harris shot her a satisfied grin. "Second of all, your fingerprints are likely all over the place considering you lived here for over ten years."

"I guess. But I never felt like it was my home." Elise followed him inside the room and gasped at the unexpected sight. "It's a freaking mess in here!"

They stood in the doorway staring at the desk scattered with open files and littered with loose papers. The coffee table was covered with empty soda cans and junk food wrappers. There were at least three empty pizza boxes on the floor, a half-eaten package of donuts on an end table, and several broken figurines lying in shards in front of the fireplace. Someone had definitely left this place in a bad mood. The only thing still intact were the books lined up on the shelves, their spines stiff as though they'd never even been opened.

"Are you sure the cops didn't execute a search warrant in here yet?" Harris asked.

"No. I think Regina must've used this room to

binge on the junk food she wouldn't allow in the rest of the house. When the housekeeper quit a couple of years ago, I took over the cleaning as a way to help around the house and keep busy in between handling the work for her fundraisers. But, like I said, I wasn't supposed to come in here by myself. Probably to give her time to get rid of evidence like this." Elise picked up an open bag of nacho-flavored chips; the only thing left inside was cheese powder dust, a lipstick-stained napkin and an empty bottle of orange soda. "You wouldn't believe how many lectures she gave me over the years about carbs and processed foods and red dyes. It never had anything to do with health and everything to do with appearance. And all along she was hiding in here and shoveling her face full of the things she'd never let me get at the store. I don't remember a pizza delivery guy ever coming to the house. And I did all the grocery shopping. Where did she even buy all of—"

"Lise?" Harris interrupted her by putting both of his hands on either side of her arms and turning her back to the desk. "Let's focus on looking for the important paperwork, okay?"

"Right." Elise gave one final glare toward the pile of empty Reese's wrappers. "She told me she was allergic to chocolate."

"Sounds like that wasn't the only thing she lied about." Harris held up a statement with the name of the same investment firm that was on the funeral company's invoice. "This says Elise Mackenzie, Beneficiary. There's a guy's name listed as the trustee. Do you know him?"

Elise looked at the spot where Harris was pointing. "Dan Russo? The name sounds familiar, but I'm not placing a face. Why is my address listed as a PO box in Raleigh? All of our mail came to the house. That's how I knew where my aunt banked."

"It's not a bank statement, though." Harris handed the document to her so she could see it better. "It's a trust. And it's in your name."

At that announcement, Elise's vision went slightly blurry. She tried to focus on the date under the mailing address—four years ago—and then everything went fuzzy again when she saw the number at the bottom.

"Are you okay?" Harris wrapped one of his arms around her waist. "Do you need to sit down?"

She used her thumb and index finger to zoom in on the paper, then realized she wasn't on her smartphone. "The date is from a few years ago, but I think I'm reading the balance wrong. What does it say?"

Harris confirmed the number and everything went blank for a second. When the world drifted back into focus, she realized that Harris was guiding her into the chair behind the desk. "Sit here," he said. "Don't move. I'm going to go grab you a glass of water."

Elise remained in her seat—even though she was pretty sure she'd just sat on half a sleeve of stale Oreo cookies—and picked up the papers closest to her. There were plenty of bills and statements in Regina's name with the now familiar red PAST DUE stamp. But only one other paper had Elise's name on it. A bank statement with the same PO box address listed on the trust. In fact, the monthly deposits matched the same deductions itemized on the trust paperwork. The withdrawals were from ATMs in various denominations.

"I have a bank account," Elise said to Harris when he returned with two bottles of water. "The day you came to help me feed the feral cats, I was so excited because I'd just deposited my first-ever paycheck into what I thought was my first-ever bank account. But it turns out, I had one all along. I mean, it's at a negative balance because it looks like the automatic transfers stopped going through in July. Right about the time Regina left town. She must've had them switched to another account."

Harris held the two documents together. "I don't think she could do that without getting permission from the executor of the trust. Let's try and find his contact information."

They spent the next hour going through all the files in the desk drawers, which were in complete disarray and covered with a sticky substance that might've been grape jelly at one point. They sorted and read and sorted and read some more. Elise went from feeling hopeful to feeling confused to feeling pissed off. "You know what, Harris? I can't even be in this room anymore, let alone this house. Let's take everything we've found with us. We can put the pieces together over dinner."

Although, truthfully, Elise didn't think she could eat a single thing. All she knew was that she had to get out of here. She had to get away from all the discrepancies and unexplained secrets. She had to get away from anything with her aunt's name on it. Her brain, as well as her stomach, was tied in knots. But Elise had promised him a meal and at the end of the day, she couldn't let him go hungry.

"I won't say no to that." Harris helped her out of the chair, and she had to dust the Oreo crumbs off her backside.

As they walked to the door, she felt something dragging along the bottom of her boot. She lifted her heel and peeled away a torn piece of paper that had adhered itself to her shoe with what might have been a squished green jelly bean.

"Are you kidding me?" Elise nearly shouted and Harris blinked, likely in shock since she never raised her voice. "Last Spring I bought a little bag of jelly beans from the store because they're my favorite candy. Regina found them and threw them in the trash. She handed me a stupid carrot and told me *that* was nature's candy. I think she went back when I wasn't in the kitchen and stole the bag out of the garbage."

Harris looked over her shoulder at the letter she was holding from the Law Offices of Dan Russo. As they read it together, Harris let out a whistle. "I don't think jelly beans were the only thing your aunt was stealing from you."

Harris felt like the biggest eavesdropper in the world as he listened to Elise's phone call, which she'd put on speaker so that she could take notes in the notepad she used for making lists. She'd called the attorney before they'd left her aunt's house but was only able to leave a message. Surprisingly, the man had called back by the time they'd driven down the street. Harris should've pulled over and walked to the back of the truck to give her privacy, but they were already on their way to Main Street Grille and he was starving.

"I've been trying to get ahold of you since your father's funeral," Dan Russo said after Elise introduced herself. "Your aunt said you were too upset to come to the reading of his will, and all the letters I sent went unanswered."

"My aunt never told me. I didn't even know he had a will. Or that I had a trust." Elise used her free hand to massage her temple. "Is there still money in it?"

The attorney laughed for what seemed like several minutes but was probably only a few seconds. "Yes, Miss Mackenzie. There's quite a bit of money in it." He named an astronomical figure that almost sent Harris veering across the double yellow line before he quickly gained control of the wheel. "Your father retained shares in Mackenzie Motors when he sold the dealerships and he added those to the second trust. The money you've been getting every month is the dividends. However, I started getting suspicious when I sent a letter on your twenty-fifth birthday asking you to come to my office. I had paperwork you needed to sign to transfer some of the assets over to you once you officially came of age, as per the conditions of the trust."

Elise shook her head. "I never got a letter. From what I can tell, my aunt opened a PO box in Raleigh for all the mail connected to this account and intercepted everything."

Harris's molars ground against each other as he held back every curse word he could think of, all of them directed at Regina Mackenzie. But he had to remind himself that none of this was his business.

"That other document you mentioned in your voicemail?" the attorney continued. "I sent one copy to you and one copy to your aunt via certified mail back in July advising that as the executor of the trust, I was temporarily stopping all transfers to your bank account until I heard from you directly and in person. Now that I know you didn't receive any of that money, I'm going to have to file charges against your aunt."

"Get in line," Elise mumbled, pinching the bridge of her nose.

"If you're available tomorrow, I'd be happy to drive out to Spring Forest and meet with you. I'm afraid that I'm going to have to ascertain for myself that you are in fact who you say you are."

"Of course," Elise said. "I'd be happy to meet with you—and I'll bring my ID. I get off work at four o'clock."

Harris did a double take at Elise and almost ran a red light. The woman had just found out that her net worth had more zeros than cats eating at the feral colony. Yet she had every intention of going into her job as though nothing had changed. Was she crazy?

"Actually," she quickly amended, probably realizing this was a bigger priority. "I'm supposed to meet my boss from my second job at a lighting warehouse after work. Do you think you could meet with me during my lunch break?"

What?

Harris tried to shake his head no at her, but she was already pulling up the calendar app on her phone. If Dan Russo was a good attorney, he'd explain to Elise that she never needed to work another day in her life.

Instead, the man agreed. "I can make that work. I look forward to finally seeing you in person. Your father was one of my favorite clients and talked about you all the time. I think he was already having memory problems by the time your mom passed away. He was aware that his condition would only deteriorate from there, so he made arrangements to sell the dealerships and retire. He wanted to spend as much time with you as possible before he had to enter assisted living."

"Wait. You mean he *knew* he was going to have to go into an assisted living center? He planned for it in advance?"

"Yes. He wanted to pick the best one that was closest to you. He prepaid at Horizons and had your aunt promise that she'd bring you every week to visit him."

Elise's intake of breath was loud and ragged. Harris had a feeling she was about to cry again. Instead, she calmly agreed on a time and place to meet the attorney the following day, then disconnected the call right as Harris pulled into a parking spot in front of Main Street Grille.

He was finally able to shift in his seat toward her. To his surprise, rather than fresh tears pooling in her eyes, the first thing he noticed was that her fingers were curled into balls of anger. "That no-good, lying, cheating snake."

"I hope you're talking about your aunt and not the attorney who just informed you that you're incredibly wealthy."

"All this time, Regina told me that she was paying for my dad's care." Her tone sounded angrier than it had been when she'd found out about the jelly beans. "That I should show some gratitude for the way she was paying all of our expenses out of the goodness of her heart. Meanwhile, she was lying about all of it even while she was stealing my money."

As painful as this betrayal must be for her, Harris was relieved Elise was finally displaying some emotion rather than hiding behind her quiet facade. He realized, though, that if they went inside the restaurant, she'd likely get flustered by all the other customers, which would only cause her to withdraw again.

He reached his arm across the seat and massaged her very tense shoulder. "Listen. Maybe it's best if we just get our food to go. You have a lot to process, and I know being in the public eye might be—"

"No. I'm hungry and I'm pissed and I don't feel like being alone right now. I also haven't had the money to afford a restaurant before now and for once, I think I'd like someone to make a meal for me." Elise was out of the truck before Harris could shut off the engine.

Okay. This was definitely a whole new side of her. One he wasn't sure how to handle. He scrambled out of his seat after her.

Elise's fury and determination only lasted until right after they were seated and the hostess handed them their menus. She whispered across the table, "I didn't know there would be so many people here for dinner. I thought it was more of a lunch place."

"We can still get the food to go if you want," he suggested. But before she could respond, a server approached their table.

"Hey, Harris." Nora, the middle-aged woman, greeted him first. To Elise she gave a simple, "Hey," making it obvious that not everyone in town knew who she or her family were. "What can I get you two started with to drink?"

He gestured at Elise to go first. Her eyes were wide and held a trace of panic. "Oh…uh… I guess I'll just have a water. And maybe a cherry cola. Oh, and if you have milkshakes, a chocolate one. You don't serve alcohol, do you?"

"We have beer and wine." Nora kept writing on her pad without missing a beat, as though it was totally normal for one person to order that many beverages.

"Wine sounds good too. I'll have one of those."

This time, the server did pause. Harris cleared

his throat. "Lise, do you want to look at the wine list and pick one?"

"Oh." She blinked twice before looking at the smaller menu he held out to her. "I don't know. Whichever one is the strongest."

"Okaaaay," Nora said before turning to Harris. "You want your usual?"

"Actually, I'm in the mood for something different tonight. Can you give us a few more minutes to look over the menu?"

"You're supposed to get the bacon cheese-burger," Elise said in an almost accusatory tone when the waitress walked away. "You said that's what you always order."

"I feel like having the chicken club. Sometimes I like to change things up a bit."

"I'm already dealing with enough change as it is." Elise's head fell back against the booth.

"Some of it is good change, though, right?"

"I guess. I mean, of course finding out I'm not completely destitute should have me jumping for joy. But it doesn't feel real yet. I can't even start thinking about what I would even do with all that money because I'm still stuck on the part where my aunt was stealing from me and lying about everything."

Her voice got louder the further she got into her rant. Several diners turned in their direction, but luckily, Elise didn't notice. She was too busy fidgeting with her silverware and twisting her paper napkin.

Harris lowered his voice. "My first suggestion would maybe be not to mention the money to anyone else just yet. You don't want people approaching you for the wrong reasons."

"Because I'm such an obvious mark?"

He reached across the table and took her hands in his. "That's not what I meant."

"No, but it goes without saying. Harris, I lived with this woman for eleven years and had no idea she was capable of this. I should've known, but I didn't. How can I make good decisions about my future when I never even saw this coming?"

He shook his head with so much force, a strand of hair tickled his forehead. "You were a kid when this started. Of course you wouldn't have expected something like this. Who would?"

"But I stayed. I could've fought harder to have a life for myself—to be allowed to go to college and start a career. I could've contacted the attorneys myself. I didn't though. It was too comfortable, too easy, for me to just kind of drift to the background and keep my walls up. I lived in a bubble with Regina controlling every aspect of my life because that was simpler than challenging her. Or standing up for myself."

The impact of Elise's self-realization was unfortunately interrupted by Nora's arrival with all four of her drinks, plus Harris's iced tea. The wait-ress looked first at Elise, then at Harris, then back at Elise. "Is now a good time to take your order or should I come back?"

"We might need a few minutes…" Harris started at the exact same time Elise said, "I'll have the Western Burger with extra bacon and a side of fries. Plus the onion rings. Maybe some potato salad if you have it. And I guess any other sides you think I should try."

"I think you're being too hard on yourself, Lise," Harris offered after Nora wrote down his substan-tially smaller order and walked away. "Your dad left you in Regina's care. He must've trusted her."

"Did he? He clearly knew better than to give her or me access to all my money at once. You heard Russo. He set up that trust *before* the memory is-sues started. Now I'm wondering what he put in his will. I never saw a copy of it. I never asked any questions. When my dad started going downhill, my aunt became even more controlling of me, ex-cluding me from any meetings about my dad's care or his accounts. I thought she was trying to shield me, but now it looks like she was trying to keep me from finding out what she was up to. How could I be so oblivious?"

"I'm not even going to try and defend that woman." Harris shrugged. "All I care about is mak-ing sure that you see yourself the way I see you.

I can't stand to watch you doubt yourself when you've proven to me and everyone else in this town exactly how capable you are."

Elise squinted across the table at him. "Why have you always been so nice to me?"

What was he going to say? He couldn't very well admit that he'd originally felt sorry for her—just like everyone else in town had. Or that he was trying to repay John Mackenzie's long-ago favor to his own father. Nobody wanted to hear that they were pitied or viewed as an obligation. His throat constricted and he swallowed down the truth. "I'm nice to everyone."

"That's true." She tilted her head to the side, and he knew she wasn't quite buying it. "But you took a chance by renting me that house and then hiring me with absolutely zero design experience."

"I take chances all the time in my line of work. It's what's made me successful this far." Lifting one hand, he brushed a loose curl from her face and spoke the truth. "I saw your potential. And my instincts are usually right."

Chapter Eleven

As soon as their food had arrived last night, Elise realized she'd ordered way too much. She'd been too angry and emotional after leaving her aunt's house to focus on her next steps. She should've gone straight home and thought everything through. Harris had even suggested as much after she'd gotten off the phone with Dan Russo. But Elise had been hell-bent and determined to prove herself in charge of her own life from that second forward. To prove herself capable of making any decision she wanted.

Unfortunately, her stomach groaned and complained all night long from the bad decisions she made in ordering nearly half the carbs on the menu—and then actually trying to eat it all. Maybe she'd been trying to finally put to rest all her thoughts these past few weeks about Harris and his rotation of side dishes. Or maybe it was seeing all those once forbidden food wrappers in her aunt's study. Ordering so much might have also been a subconscious *screw you* to Regina.

Either way, Elise had acted like Mr. Chow's cat Dimples last night, gorging herself on plates of food just to prove she could. She certainly didn't feel any more in control of her life or her sodium levels the following morning when she showed up for her shift at Barkyard Boarding.

In fact, she was still feeling bloated when she left on her lunch break and drove to the bank to meet Dan Russo. When she saw the distinguished older gentlemen with a well-trimmed silver beard and shiny bald head, she immediately recognized him.

"Now I remember you!" She smiled as she shook his hand. "The name didn't click right away, but I remember driving to your house in a brand-new Mercedes AMG convertible. I was nine, I think. My dad let me help put the big white bow on the hood because it was a birthday gift for your wife."

"That's right," the attorney chuckled. "Your parents knew I'd forgotten our anniversary a couple of months before and your mom told him to make me pay sticker price for that thing. My wife, Marie, still tells people it was the best present I ever gave her."

"Thank you for coming all the way out here." Elise discreetly glanced at the large clock over the entrance to the bank. "I'm sorry to be in such a rush, but I only have forty-five minutes before I'm supposed to be back at work. What do you need from me to verify my identity?"

"The notary public will need your driver's license and fingerprint, but I knew who you were the second I saw you pull up in that wood-paneled minivan. Your mother wasn't much of a car person and that was the one and only vehicle she ever allowed John Mackenzie to buy her."

"It was also the only one I wouldn't let my aunt sell when she sent the others to auction." Elise had been hoping to avoid any tears, especially out here on a very public street. Yet she found herself on the verge of sobbing, telling her father's longtime friend a summarized version of everything her aunt had lied about. "So basically, all I have to my name is some hand-me-down clothes and this minivan."

"Well, that's definitely not *all* you have to your name. And not all the cars went to auction either. At least not the ones your dad put in the trust." Mr. Russo held up his leather briefcase. "Let's go inside and we can review all the assets and start getting things transferred into your name."

Thirty minutes later, Elise realized she was never

going to be done in time to make it back to work. She excused herself from the bank manager's office to go outside and call Shane. She still hadn't told anyone other than Harris about this recent financial development, but her boss didn't ask for an explanation when she said she had a personal emergency.

"Take the rest of the afternoon off," Shane said over the barking in the background. "In fact, one of the new college students I hired was hoping to pick up more hours and would jump at the chance to cover the rest of your shift—or even more. I meant to bring it up earlier, to let you know that you won't be leaving us in the lurch if Harris needs you full-time."

"Thanks," Elise said before disconnecting. She doubted Harris needed her at all, though, even after he gave her that line last night about taking a chance on her because he saw her potential.

She'd seen what had looked like guilt flash across his face right before he'd said it. It was tough to tell if Harris had been holding something back or if Elise was just expecting another betrayal.

Signing all the paperwork and setting up the wire transfers to her new account took most of the afternoon. It hadn't helped that the bank manager had announced to every employee who walked by his office that "Miss Mackenzie is one of our most valuable customers."

Was this how people were going to start treating her when they found out about her inheritance? Fawning over her? Pretending she wasn't the same person they'd deemed ineligible for a savings account last week unless she could maintain a fifty-dollar balance in it at all times? She'd rather go back to everyone ignoring her because they thought she was broke.

"Could my client and I have a moment alone?" Dan Russo finally said to the bank manager.

When there was nobody else in the room, the attorney motioned for Elise to come stand near the window with him. His voice was calm and reassuring as he spoke.

"Do you see all the people on the sidewalk out there? All the cars? All the shops and restaurants?" he asked, waiting for her to nod in response. "The rest of the world is going to go on the way it always does whether Elise Mackenzie is rich or poor. Some might treat you differently, but at the end of the day, the only life this inheritance has the power to change is yours. And only if you let it. I have clients who want to hide money from their spouses, and I have clients who set up irrevocable trusts that the beneficiaries can never change. But this one is set up to allow you to control your destiny. Your father used to call you his little shadow. All those times you were following him around, sticking close to his side, he was studying you too. He told me that you were shy, just like your mother. But you were also a deep thinker, just like him. He spent more time with you than anyone else and I truly believe he knew exactly what he was doing when he put all this responsibility in your hands."

Elise's rib cage grew tighter as both doubt and hope battled inside her chest. She shoved her hands into the back pockets of her jeans and asked, "If my dad was *that* sure of me and *that* astute with money, then why did he choose Regina as my guardian?"

"Your aunt wasn't always the selfish and grasping person that she became. Just like everyone, she was shaped by her choices—and she made some very bad ones. My guess is she made some reckless investments after your uncle died that wiped out her personal wealth. But she couldn't admit that her money was gone. Not when she'd gotten used to the respect and prestige that came from her position in society. So she became desperate to maintain appearances—at any cost."

It was true. The Regina she'd lived with over the past several years valued image more than anything else. Still, there had been some good times back when Elise had been a little girl visiting her aunt and uncle. Maybe she shouldn't be so focused on only the bad.

"Now—" Dan Russo put a paternal arm over Elise's shoulders "—my advice to you is the same thing I'd tell one of my own children in this situation. Take some time to let everything sink in. Don't be in a hurry to jump into any big decisions."

Elise's stomach growled, reminding her that she hadn't eaten since her last big decision, which had caused her to overindulge. The lawyer politely ignored the sound.

"None of this stuff—" he handed her a file labeled *Assets* "—is going anywhere. We can deal with it whenever you feel up to it or just keep things the way they are. Call me if you need anything, or even if you just want to talk about your dad. I have a lot of stories."

When he put out his hand to shake hers again, she pulled the older man in for a hug. Between Dan Russo and Simon Vega, she hadn't felt this connected to her father in years. Elise made a mental promise to herself that she wouldn't close herself off again from people like this.

She left the bank that afternoon more wealthy and more confused than she'd ever been. She was only a few steps away from her minivan when one of the tellers, the one who had also acted as the notary public, came running after her.

"Excuse me, Miss Mackenzie." The woman was out of breath by the time she'd caught up and Elise braced herself to hear that there had been a terrible mistake and she'd have to return all the money. Instead, the woman said, "I didn't want to bring this up in front of my manager, but is it too late to register my pet for the fashion show next week? You guys allow guinea pigs, right?"

Relief washed over Elise and suddenly the world made sense again.

She gave the bank teller one of the flyers from her tote bag, then got behind the wheel of her ancient, but well-loved minivan.

See. She could still be herself, still organize the animal shelter fundraiser and still meet Harris at The Lighting District. Oh crap. She was supposed to be there in five minutes.

Elise dug around in her bag for the banana she'd grabbed this morning on her way out the door and ate it as she drove to a big shopping center on the other side of town. Walking across the parking lot to the front of the store, she checked her phone. After Harris had dropped her off at her car last night, they hadn't confirmed exactly where to meet today. He might've shown up at Barkyard to pick her up again.

There were no new notifications, though. And no sign of him at the entrance. She shot him a text. I'm here.

Where? was his only reply.

At The Lighting District. I thought we were meeting at 4?

You're kidding!

Why would she joke about a business meeting? She typed as much and pressed Send before realizing her tone could've come across as annoyed. So Elise did something she'd never done.

She took a selfie.

Okay, so it was only about three-fourths of her face in the frame with the store's overhead sign the primary focus in the background. Roxy would have to teach her how to manage a better angle, but it still counted as a selfie. With a giggle she barely recognized, Elise pressed Send.

The three dots flashed on the screen indicating Harris was typing, but then they quickly disappeared. Another few minutes went by with no response. The daring excitement she'd felt a few moments ago suddenly turned to dread. Maybe she'd misunderstood something. Maybe the selfie had made her seem a bit too desper—

The sound of a horn interrupted her thoughts and made her look out toward the street just in time to see Harris's blue work truck make an illegal left turn into the parking lot. Thankfully, his speed reduced as he approached the other cars and pedestrians.

"Sorry I'm late," he said as he took long strides toward her. Man, he could cover some distance when he was in a hurry. "I didn't think you were coming."

"Why would you think that? Didn't we agree we

needed to get the light fixtures picked out before the electricians come tomorrow?"

He shoved a hand through his dark messy hair, making his wide smile and chambray work shirt compete for whatever was left of her attention span. All the blood in her body rushed to her head. Or her heart. Or possibly somewhere farther down. Somehow, he got better looking every time she saw him.

"Yeah, but that was before you found out about your…you know…*meeting* with your attorney."

"That doesn't change anything, Harris. I still have a job to do. Right?"

He didn't respond right away, and her earlier desire turned to dismay. "Actually, I was thinking about that today."

Elise's mouth dropped open, and she had to snap it closed so she could form the dreaded question. "You mean you're firing me?"

"No!" Harris accidentally shouted a bit too loudly, causing a customer leaving the store to stare at them. He scratched the back of his neck, realizing that this probably wasn't the best place to tell her his idea. "Come on, let's go inside so we can talk while we look at lights."

Except Elise kept her feet planted where they were.

"Or I guess we can discuss it out here with everyone walking by." Harris rubbed a hand across the lower half of his face, wishing he'd remembered to shave this morning. "So I was thinking about what you said a few weeks ago. About how there was this power imbalance between us since I was the boss, and you were the employee."

"You're going to fire me over that?" Again, she spoke right as another customer came outside. But this particular person was much nosier than the last and stopped his cart to openly stare at them.

"Nobody is firing anybody," Harris said first to Elise and then more forcefully a second time to the stranger who was watching them. When the man finally walked away—quite slowly—Harris continued his explanation. "I was simply thinking Vega Homes would go in a different direction. Rather than employing a part-time designer, I thought we could contract the work out to an independent firm. Personally, I think Elise Mackenzie Interiors has a nice ring to it, but obviously you could pick whatever company name you like."

Elise took a step back. "But maybe I don't want to run my own business. I mean, at least not yet. I'd want to get a business degree, figure out accounting and marketing and all the rest of it. For now, I was thinking that I could just keep doing this until I figure out what I want."

"Of course you should go for a degree if that's what you want, but you don't need that before you start a business. You'd be doing exactly the same thing you're doing now, except you'd be your own boss. That's the best part of my plan. Actually, the second best." Another customer walked out. This time an older woman. "The real best part would be that you could feel free to make out with me on the jobsite whenever you wanted. Oh, so *now* you want to talk about it inside?"

Elise whirled around long enough to flash him a disapproving look that would've been a bit more intimidating if her cheeks weren't quite so pink. He held back his laughter as he followed her into The Lighting District and down one of the first empty aisles.

"You should've brought a cart," she said when he finally caught up to her. "Because now that I'm your independently contracted design consultant, I plan to spend a whole lot more of your money."

That wiped the smile off his face.

She handed him two boxes containing wall sconces. "How about instead of starting the conversation by making me think you're firing me, you ask me if I'd be interested in running my own business?"

"Fair enough." He tucked one box under each arm. "Let me try that again. Hey, Lise, what do you think of the idea of starting your own design firm? I just closed escrow on that brick Tudor and have another listing I want you to see. I know you like working with the animals at Barkyard Boarding, so I'd hate for you to think I'm trying to steal you away from Shane. It's just that I need you more than he does."

As soon as the words were out of his mouth, he replayed them in his mind hoping they didn't sound like he meant he needed her in the emotional sense rather than the business sense. Really, it was both when it came down to it, but he had a feeling that saying so aloud would send her running to her car.

"How do you know I want to keep working at all?" She handed him a pendant light.

"Because you were pissed off earlier when you thought I was going to fire you." He winked in response to her scowl. "I told you I had good instincts, just bad timing sometimes with my lines. What's this for?"

"The kitchen island. We're going to need three more, so you might want to find a cart before you run out of hands."

He left and returned with two shopping carts.

"For the record," she said as she passed him the other pendant lights, "I do want to keep working. For now, at least. Dan Russo told me today that I should take my time and not rush into any decisions. I don't want the money to change me and the best way to do that is for me to stay busy."

"That shouldn't be a problem considering how much you already have going on with the fundraiser, your work with me and your second job at Barkyard."

"My *second job*? I thought working with *you* was my second job." Elise corrected him without taking her eyes off the display of a modern and sleek gold-plated vanity light. "This would be perfect for the downstairs bathroom, but I'm not seeing any in stock."

Harris frowned at the display. "Are you sure? I thought we were doing the navy blue cabinets in there."

"We are. But the gold will bring out the geometric pattern in the wallpaper and help tie it all together. Trust me."

So far, she hadn't steered him wrong on her accent choices. "Fine. We can order that vanity light if they can get it to us before the end of the week."

They continued down each aisle, slowly filling the carts while Elise added ideas to her notepad for the other houses he was flipping. Harris had thought she was pretty before, but by the time they got to the chandeliers, he couldn't take his eyes off her. It could've been the warm-lit ambiance in this section or it could've been her decisive take-charge attitude. But Elise Mackenzie had to be the most beautiful woman he'd ever seen.

It wasn't until they arrived at the ceiling fans when she finally asked, "Why do you keep staring at me?"

"Because I can't stop." He smoothed back one of the loose waves that had fallen from her ponytail. But the air circulating from the fans above wouldn't let it stay in place. "And because I'm waiting for you to decide when you're going to kiss me again."

He was rewarded with twin spots of pink on both of her cheeks. He lifted his other hand to cup the opposite side of her face and felt her shiver.

"You know—" Harris lowered his voice "—the past few weeks I've been trying to be patient. To not rush you. And you know I'm not the slowest mover when it comes to going after what I want. So far, though, I think I've done a pretty good job of keeping my hands to myself. But it's getting more and more difficult not to stare at you."

Elise's lips opened slightly, all but begging him to kiss her. But no matter how much he wanted to close the short distance between them, he wasn't going to break that promise. Instead, he kept talking. "I know you liked kissing me, Lise. I know you'll like doing other stuff with me too. If we ever get to that point, which I hope we will. But I want you to want it. I don't want you to have regrets."

"Harris," she started, then quickly looked away. He held still, though, watching her chest rise and fall with her short breaths until she finally returned his gaze. "I don't have much experience with relationships or even the physical stuff really."

"That's what you said about being a designer, but

you've more than proved yourself capable in that department. I think you're capable of a lot more than you realize. Maybe we could start with one of your lists. What's the first thing you'd like to accomplish?"

Her hands lifted to his chest and all the muscles in his arms strained as he held himself in place, refusing to give in to his urge to haul her all the way against him. Her voice was whispery soft when she said, "This."

Elise's lips pressed against his lightly at first, and then with more pressure. Harris shoved his fingers deeper into her hair and she wrapped her arms around his neck before opening her mouth to him.

Kissing Elise was as natural as breathing, but it was also as intoxicating as having pure oxygen flowing directly into his lungs. His hands moved to her waist, and he pulled her tighter to him. She was tiny in his arms, but apparently with legs long enough that her hips aligned perfectly with his. Harris eased his palms lower, cupping the round curves of her—

"Attention Lighting District shoppers." The startling blare of the overhead speakers reminded them where they were. "We will be closing in five minutes."

Elise swore softly and Harris held back his laughter by looking away from her obviously swollen lips. When he moved his gaze downward, he took one look at her feet and a snickering sound escaped the back of his throat.

"What's so funny?" she asked, her creased brow right at his eye level.

"When we were kissing, it seemed like you were taller, but I was too absorbed in the moment to wonder why." He nodded at the wood pallet she was standing on—several boxes of ceiling fans stacked behind her. "Now I know why."

Someone cleared their throat and Harris looked over Elise's shoulder to see an employee in a bright green vest averting their gaze. "We're…uh…closing soon, folks. Is there anything I can help you find?"

Elise squeaked before burying her face in Harris's shoulder.

"Nope." Harris kept his arms around her waist. "We already have everything we need right here."

Chapter Twelve

"You probably don't require my assistance at the check-out line," Elise told Harris, her face burning with embarrassment at being caught making out in a public store. Or maybe it was just the lingering heat from Harris's very thorough and very talented kiss. "I'll just meet you in the parking lot and help you load everything."

"Oh no." Harris grabbed her hand before she could get away. "You're not running off on me again. Besides, I can't remember the bathroom vanity light you wanted to order. You'd hate to end up with that silver mosaic one."

"Fine," she said, which came out more as a

growl. "But only because a delay in getting the right materials could set the whole schedule back."

Thankfully, the cashier was a different employee than the one who'd busted them a few minutes ago and Elise's blush had faded to a much more normal shade by the time they pushed their loaded carts outside.

She saw the warehouse store across the parking lot with its lights on and drew to a stop in front of Harris. "Do you think Stone and Slab is still open?"

Harris's breath behind her ear was warm and sent a shiver racing down her spine. "Why? Is that the second thing on your list? To see what happens when I kiss you with a countertop nearby instead of just a pallet?"

The heat that shot through her wasn't embarrassment this time. It was pure desire. She was supposed to be taking life slowly and not making any rash decisions. But in less than two hours with the impulsive Harris Vega, she'd already founded her own design consulting business and started a hypothetical list of steps to take their relationship to the physical level.

Maybe she should just sleep with the guy and get it over with. At the same time, though, she'd be full of regret if things changed between them. The only way she could guarantee that her life didn't get too out of whack was by sticking to business as usual. And by remaining in control of the situation. "Let's put this stuff in the car and then try to find something for the kitchen island at Stone and Slab. The cabinets are going in on Monday and with the pet fashion show on Saturday, my schedule is going to be tight. But we're only *looking* at countertops, Harris. Not, you know, trying them out."

He threw back his head to laugh, the warm tan skin of his exposed neck all but begging her to kiss it. Stay focused, she told herself, trying to ignore the throbbing ache still lingering from their unfinished kiss.

In the end, they found the perfect slab of Corsica marble that was also discounted since it was the last piece. Of course, it took longer to find since they got distracted with more kisses near the quartz samples, had a few heated embraces in the tile section and couldn't keep their hands off each other by the time they made it to the granite.

"You want to grab a bite to eat?" Harris asked as they held hands on their way to their cars.

Her stomach growled. Up until he'd mentioned food, she'd forgotten that all she'd had so far today was a banana. But she also had a ton of fundraising emails to reply to and she'd promised Buster that she'd try to recreate his late mom's peanut butter cookie recipe. It would be easy enough to invite Harris over for dinner since she'd already prepped this weeks' meals. But after the way her body had reacted to him in public stores, she didn't think she could trust herself with him in the privacy of her own home.

"I better not. I have a lot to catch up on before the pet fashion show. More than a lot. But it's good. I need to stay busy. Do I sound nervous about it? I know I start rattling on and on when I'm nervous. Which is weird because most people think I never talk. Gah, I'm even doing it now. Okay, I'm done."

"It's going to be amazing." Harris squeezed her hand. "I was at Furever Paws this morning checking on the footings we used for the runway. Bunny told me that one of the pets walking that night will be a potbellied pig, so we had to make some adjustments for the weight capacity."

"Uh-oh. I hadn't thought about that being an issue." Elise scrunched her face, then began searching in her bag for her notepad as she spoke. "Do your changes affect the overall size? Because I might have to order another red carpet. They're harder to find than you'd think since they have to look real, but still be easily cleaned if one of the animals accidentally takes a—"

"Lise." Harris lifted her chin. "I'll text you the new measurements. If anyone can find that stain resistant pet-friendly red carpet, it's you. Get home to make your calls and return your emails. And don't worry about me. I should have things covered at the jobsites until after the fashion show gets wrapped up. This list we started between us tonight—" he dropped a soft kiss on her lips "—will still be here next week. Call me if you need anything."

Then he did the best thing he could've possibly done in that moment. He got in his truck, and he got out of her way. Elise worked better without distractions and right now, Harris Vega with his sexy grin and knowing eyes and skilled kisses was a huge distraction.

Of course, the man was never far from her mind the rest of the week as she spent most of her time either running errands or at the shelter making last-minute adjustments to the schedule and the decorations. A smaller —and more welcomed—distraction was little Pancake, the puppy who always knew when Elise was somewhere nearby.

"We really would like to get her socialized a bit more," Birdie said before handing Elise one of the newly donated halters and leashes. "We're still waiting on the cardiologist to give us the go-ahead on her health condition to see if she's strong enough to be spayed, but if everything goes according to plan, Pancake might be available for adoption as soon as next week."

Elise didn't really mind the extra babysitting task, especially since Shane had given her the rest of the week off to focus on the fundraiser. She liked working at Barkyard, but it was clear that there were plenty of newer employees who needed the hourly wage more than she did now. She wasn't supposed to be making any big changes yet, but maybe it was time to let her first job go.

"And just between us girls," Elise said to Pancake as they walked outside to where the giant tent was being erected. "I really like the idea of having my own design firm. Although, I'm still not entirely convinced I know what I'm doing."

Pancake swished her fluffy tail back and forth when it was just her and Elise. But anytime one of the other volunteers came to ask where she wanted something, the puppy would duck between her feet.

"You're still a shy little thing," she told the pup later in the afternoon. "But at least you're not tiring yourself out and making me carry you everywhere."

On Friday morning, Bethany handed Elise a cup of coffee. "I just got a call from the audio tech people. They want to know if you'd prefer a handheld mic or if you want a clip-on one tomorrow."

Elise's hairline shot up. "Why would I need a mic?"

"Because you're going to be the master of ceremonies for the fashion show?" Rebecca made the statement sound more like a question.

"But doesn't the emcee do most of the talking? Out loud? With everyone watching them? I kinda figured I'd be more behind the scenes the whole time. Making sure everything runs smoothly."

Bethany looked around at the nonstop activity surrounding them. "Then who would be the emcee?"

Elise gulped. "I guess I assumed someone who works here would do it."

"I'm stationed at the silent auction tables and Bunny and Birdie are going to be backstage in case any of the animals need to be separated. Doc J has terrible stage fright and most of the volunteers are either participating in the show with their pets or were hoping to watch. Since Regina had planned to do it before she went AWOL, I figured you were planning to take over that part."

It was true. Elise *had* intended to follow through on all the elaborate plans her aunt had promised. But she hadn't intended to be the actual host. "The thing is," Elise started, then took a sip of coffee to fortify her nerves. "I'm not really much of a public speaker."

Bethany didn't look surprised by the admission. Obviously, most people who spent even a few minutes with Elise wouldn't be shocked to learn that. Still, the shelter director grinned encouragingly.

"You know what's going on backward and forward, Elise. You know all the donors and all the entrants in the fashion show. You even came up with the script. All you would need to do is read it. You wouldn't even be on stage that much. We can put a podium off to the side. Besides, everyone's attention is going to be on the animals walking the runway."

Okay. She could do this, she told herself the rest of the day anytime doubt crept in. But that evening when she got home, she dropped her bag and keys on the table and said to the empty kitchen, "I can't do this."

Her phone rang and she saw Harris's name on the screen. They'd talked or texted a few times throughout the week whenever he had a question about a jobsite or whenever she had a question about changing the layout of the stage. Even though he'd been trying not to be a distraction, he'd still made himself available, which she appreciated.

"Hello?" she answered.

"Hey, I just got to Furever Paws and saw these notes you left about the runway. Making the risers are no problem for the floor lighting, but the plants Buster found at the landscape place are way too tall. They're going to block the view for the people in the first row."

"Okay. Then just put them along the back side of the tent for now. I'll take a look at them tomorrow and find a place where we can incorporate them."

"Roger that. How're you holding up, Lise? You sound tired."

She told Harris about the evening's lack of a master of ceremonies. "I know it's ultimately my responsibility because I didn't think to line anyone else up. But I don't think I can do it."

She expected him to give her the same pep talk Bethany had earlier. Instead, he asked, "Are you somewhere with good Wi-Fi?"

"Um, yeah. I'm at home. Why?"

"Because my dad sent me some videos he'd found online the other day and wanted me to show you. It's a large file so I'm going to send it now."

"That's thoughtful of your dad, Harris, but I really won't have the time to download anything until after Saturday."

"Just watch one," Harris said. "I promise it's not another video of Igor sunning himself on their front porch. Or one of the links to my mom's favorite cooking with Broadway stars podcasts."

"Fine." As soon as Elise disconnected the call, her phone pinged with a notification of a new video.

She tapped the download icon and, within a minute, her father's face filled her screen. Elise gasped and nearly dropped her phone. But her dad's voice continued, "Are you looking for a new car? Well, look no further than Mackenzie Motors, where making deals is what we do best."

It was one of John Mackenzie's first commercials, his hair still the same dark brown as Elise's before he'd eventually gone gray. Later on, Mackenzie Motors had been well-known for their zany advertisements and spoofs on pop culture, but even in the early ads, which were much simpler in setup, his charisma shone through. Her father had a larger-than-life personality and people had always gravitated toward him. It was what made him such a successful salesman.

She'd promised to watch only one, but each video was funnier and more outlandish than the last one. Now *this* was the father she'd wanted to remember, the man he was before Alzheimer's had stolen him from her.

His zest for life had been contagious and his ability to laugh at himself often put others at ease. Elise spent the next hour sitting in her kitchen watching grainy footage of her dad dressed up like eighties icons, shooting himself out of a cannon, and even riding through a row of cars on an elephant. In another commercial, the one where he was dancing next to a giant slot machine, she could've sworn she saw her mother in the background dressed like a Las Vegas showgirl. Elise replayed the video several times, each time becoming more and more convinced that the person in the elaborate sequined headpiece was in fact Eleanor Mackenzie, her very shy and very introverted mother.

She immediately sent Harris a text. Will you ask your dad if my mom was ever in any of the Mackenzie Motors commercials?

Elise walked to the bathroom to take a shower, but before she could get to the hallway, she had her answer. Dad said she was in almost all of them, although you can't always tell it's her. Like when she wore the chicken costume.

Elise went through all the videos again, spotting her mother somewhere in the background almost every time, usually as an extra, always in some kind of costume. Her father could negotiate just about anything, but how in the world had he talked his wife—who some might have said was even more quiet and reserved than Elise—into going on television?

A childhood memory popped into her mind. It had been late at night, after Elise had already had her bath and bedtime story. She'd woken up and wanted a glass of water. When she went downstairs, her dad was sitting in his favorite leather chair and her mom had been sitting on his lap, holding a giant sketchpad. *"When the genie comes out of the bottle and asks for your three wishes, you describe the new car models on the lot."*

"Sounds like another winner to me, Eleanor," her dad said before picking up his wife and spinning her around in his arms. *"You'll play the genie, right?"*

Elise had been five or six at the time and happily oblivious to anything but their joy. She'd run up to them to join in whatever they'd been excited about and her parents had laughed and pulled her into the family hug.

Now, she sat on her bed, scrolling through the videos until she found the one her mom had described in Elise's memory. There it was. Except her mom wasn't the genie, she was one of the dancing flying carpets in the background.

Elise fell back against her pillows, smiling at her mother's ingenuity. Eleanor Mackenzie had found a way to overcome her shyness and carve out a role for herself in her husband's business and his life.

Well, hell. If her introverted mother could dress up in a chicken costume on national television, surely Elise could emcee a little fundraiser in Spring Forest.

The only difference was nobody would be able to hide in the background this time.

People were already arriving to the pet fashion show and Harris couldn't find Elise anywhere.

"You gonna tell her tonight?" Buster asked as they centered the final red carpet at the end of the runway.

"Probably not." Harris stood up and straightened his sport coat. "She's already got a lot to think about and I don't want to take away from her big night."

"I get that. But it's kinda a big deal to land the cover of *Coming Home*. It could be sort of a double celebration for you guys."

"I'm not sure. Lise is the quiet, reserved type and might not want to have her name or picture splashed

CHRISTY JEFFRIES

235

all over one of the most popular magazines in the country. She prefers to stay behind the scenes."

Buster's attention turned to something on the stage behind Harris and the foreman chuckled. "Well, she's certainly not staying behind the scenes tonight."

Harris's lungs seized as he saw Elise walking down the runway toward them. Her silky brown hair was down in long loose waves and her dress was... Whoa. He had to blink several times so his eyes could adjust to the deep plunge of the silky black fabric outlining her small round breasts. The cocktail dress was fitted to the waist before flaring out and hitting just below her thighs. Her bare, toned legs were everything he'd imagined they'd be as she strode across the stage in her high heels.

The air grew thicker the closer she came, and Harris was afraid he was standing there with his tongue hanging out, similar to many of the actual canines that would be in attendance tonight.

"Did the lighting turn out the way you wanted?" Buster asked, clearly not as affected as Harris, who couldn't form so much as a greeting.

Elise smiled and—wow. Okay. Red lipstick. He was not expecting that. "It looks even better than I hoped."

"*You* look even better," Harris started before realizing how weird and possibly insulting it sounded. "I mean you look amazing. But not better. You're always beautiful no matter what you wear, but that dress is, um, definitely different than your jeans. Which I also like. Man, I sound like an idiot and need to just shut up. Are you wearing earrings?"

Elise's hand flew to her ear. "Oh, yes. Roxy, the girl across the street, helped me get ready. She needed a ride to the mall to pick out her shoes for homecoming, which I think was just a trick to get me to buy this whole outfit. She did my hair and makeup too. I think she's seen one too many make-over movies. You don't think I look too extra, do you?"

Harris shook his head quickly. "I think you look absolutely perfect."

Her smile was as bright as the lights shining up at them on the stage. "You clean up pretty nicely yourself."

His hand went to the open collar of his dress shirt. "Be sure to tell my mom that when she gets here. I own *one* tie, which she bought for me, and I couldn't find it anywhere because I haven't had a chance to sort through my stuff since hauling it over for my stay at another remodel. Don't tell her that either. She doesn't get why a man who has so many houses doesn't actually live in any of them."

"I already saw your dad backstage with Igor, so I'll keep an eye out for her. I have to go do a sound check now. Where will you be sitting?"

"Probably on this side somewhere." Harris pointed to a row of chairs. "Why?"

Elise bit her lower lip. "If I mess up my lines, I'm going to need to spot a reassuring face in the crowd."

"You won't mess up," he said before wrapping one hand around her waist. "But just in case, here's a kiss for good luck."

His lips had barely connected with hers when a little bark sounded below them. "Enough of that, you two," Bunny Whitaker said. "We've got money to raise and animals to socialize. Here, Harris, you take Pancake. She's not available for adoption just yet, but she's an adorable walking advertisement for what we do here at Furever Paws."

More like a *carrying* advertisement, Harris realized after Bunny left and he had to scoop the puppy into his arms. He'd heard that Elise was the only one who could get Pancake to follow on the leash.

As more people filed into the seats surrounding the stage, Harris caught up with friends and even did a little networking with some business associates. But he tried not to stray too far in case Elise needed him. When the music started, though, he took his seat and soon realized that she had everything under control. In fact, her descriptions of the animals walking the runway were clever and witty and she kept the pace flowing, even when the models failed to follow their handlers or when a pygmy goat dressed in a basketball uniform proved that it wasn't quite housebroken yet.

"That's okay, Peanut," Elise announced as the goat's owner led it offstage and one of the volunteers standing by for this exact reason quickly cleaned up the mess. "Even GOATs like Michael Jordan have to leave the court at halftime for a bathroom break. Next up we have Pepper, a black Labrador, being escorted by Abby and Annie."

Elise gave an encouraging smile to the two-and-a-half-year-old twins, who walked on either side of the dog they'd dressed in a pink tutu. Harris spotted Ian and Rachel in the audience watching their girls, the pride evident on their faces.

Then came Simon Vega, holding Igor on a pillow sewn to look like a rock. Apparently, Harris's mom had no trouble getting the bearded dragon into the cactus costume she'd made for him.

Wendy, one of his tenants, finished off the show with her boyfriend's working dog, Jedi, whose service vest had been spruced up with colorful beads and crystals. Greg Martin was waiting for them at the end of the runway and lifted his girlfriend off the stage and into his arms.

"We want to thank everyone for coming out tonight to support Furever Paws. But the fun isn't over just yet," Elise announced as she took the stage with one of the corporate sponsors. "Feline Finest is here to help us announce the winners of the cutest pet contest."

Igor did not win Coolest Reptile, which came as no surprise to Harris. But the animals who did win their categories received their prizes before the corporate sponsor presented Elise with a huge cardboard check that was nearly as big as she was.

"Thank you to all the donors tonight," Elise said, generating a loud round of applause. "We couldn't have done this without the generosity of the entire community and a terrific crew of volunteers. Now, we hope everyone sticks around to enjoy the food provided by Josie's Catering and the live music provided by Big Kitty and the Strays. Also, the silent auction is still open for another hour and don't worry if you forgot your checkbooks at home, folks. We're happy to take cash, credit cards and online payments."

As the audience filtered out to the pavilion, where the after-party was in full swing, Harris waited patiently near the stage steps, Pancake still in his arms.

"You did amazing," he told Elise as she carefully descended in her extremely high heels. Harris's cheeks hurt from grinning so much and his chest stretched to its limits with pride. The puppy began to squirm and practically leaped toward Elise, trying to lick her face. "Even Pancake stayed awake the whole time, that's how entertaining she thought you were."

Elise took the bundle of fur from him, placing a kiss between the dog's ears. "Is that right? Was it *me* who held your attention or was it those chickens Tony brought out in that decorated wagon?"

"Well, it certainly wasn't Mr. Chow's cat. She nearly crawled inside my sport coat when Dimples was on the stage."

"You were fantastic," Shane said to Elise as he approached them. He was carrying his one-year-old son, Wyatt, who immediately put out a pudgy hand to grab one of Pancake's ears. "Who knew my shy former employee could work a crowd like that? Bethany and I might need to lock you in as the emcee for the Christmas wedding we're planning."

"Congratulations," Elise started just as Harris realized what Shane had said.

"Wait?" Harris shook his head. "*Former* employee?"

Elise set Pancake on the ground, out of Wyatt's curious reach. "With all the extra hours I was putting in for the fundraiser and working for you, it seemed only fair that I let one of the newer employees at Barkyard take over my shifts. But Shane said I can still come visit some of my favorites at doggy day care."

Wow. Harris felt all the blood rush to his head.

"This means that once the fundraiser is officially over, I'll have you all to myself?"

Shane lifted his eyebrows, but was polite enough to excuse himself. "I better take Wyatt over to see Peanut, the goat. He loves the farm animals."

"You'll have all of my *design services* to yourself," she corrected once Shane left. "Until I start taking on more clients, that is. Or unless I'm busy feeding your crew or my feral cat colony."

Pancake followed beside Elise as she set off toward the after-party. Oh sure, *now* the puppy walked on its leash. Harris quickly caught up.

"What do you mean *your* feral cat colony?"

"I asked Dan Russo to draw up an offer on the Maple Street property."

"But that house isn't for sale yet. I haven't even had time to fix up the kitchen like I promised you."

"I know, but I figured it would help even the playing field between us if I was no longer your tenant. Plus, I like the place and the neighbors. The house itself needs more work, but it feels like home to me."

For someone who didn't want to make a lot of changes, it sure felt as though everything was moving all at once. While Harris appreciated Elise's growing confidence, he couldn't help the uneasy feeling in his gut or the need to slow things down long enough to make sense out of all these recent developments. All he could say was, "I've never sold a house that isn't finished."

Elise turned toward him, her smile nearly taking the air right out of his lungs. "I've never done a lot of things either. So I guess we're both learning to adapt to new experiences."

Clearly, though, one of them was doing better in that regard. People came up to Elise all evening, telling her how much they'd enjoyed the fashion show and how great everything had turned out. She smiled and nodded and made conversation, but she stayed close enough to Harris's side that he could still see the tension in her body and her face as she fought the urge to retreat into her quiet comfort zone.

When she had to announce the last call for the silent auction, Harris offered to take Pancake out to a grassy area to relieve herself. When he returned, Elise was huddled with Bethany and the bid sheets, going over the final numbers.

"I can't believe how much we brought in," Bethany told Elise. "I don't think any of our past fundraisers have been this successful."

"That's why I had to make myself scarce," a voice said behind Harris, causing Elise to gasp. "I knew the only way we could pull off something this big was if I motivated my niece to get out on her own and prove to herself that she could be just as successful as me."

Regina Mackenzie stood there in her party dress and flawless makeup, not a hair or jewel out of place. The uninvited and unapologetic woman even had the audacity to smile as she spoke with the most condescending tone Harris had ever heard. "I'm so glad everything worked out according to my plan."

Chapter Thirteen

"What are you doing here?" Elise asked her aunt. She should've been shocked, but it somehow seemed inevitable that Regina Mackenzie would show up at the last possible minute and take credit for everything. It was what the woman had done as far back as Elise could remember.

Normally, she'd be politely accepting all the possible excuses Aunt Regina could dig up, but tonight, Elise no longer cared. She was too angry. Too ashamed.

"You didn't think I would miss the biggest event of the year, did you?" Regina gave a finger wave to someone in the distance. Elise turned in time to see the mayor and several local business owners redirect their gazes to avoid making eye contact with the notorious socialite.

"That's exactly what I thought," Elise admitted. "I'd even hoped that you would stay long gone this time. But that's only something a rational and self-aware person would do, and you've proven yourself to be neither of those things. Please stop waving at the other guests. Do you seriously think there is anyone here tonight who is still willing to be associated with you after the scandal you've caused?"

"What scandal?" Regina's attempt at a jovial laugh was way too forced and grated on Elise's already raw nerves.

Tightly holding Pancake's leash in one hand, Elise consciously forced herself to unclench her opposite fingers from the fist they'd formed, resisting the urge to knock that fake smile off her aunt's face. "You stole money from this fundraiser and then skipped town, Regina. It's not a secret."

"Don't be ridiculous." Regina sniffed, her cheerful facade slipping. "Why would I need to steal money from some rinky-dink animal shelter?"

Bethany gasped, reminding Elise that there was now an entire audience of people watching the interaction. She straightened her shoulders, choosing her next words carefully.

But before Elise could voice them, Harris placed himself between the two women. "Probably for the same reason you've been stealing your niece's inheritance all these years while playing the role of generous benefactor."

This time, the gasps were louder and echoed throughout the entire crowd. So much for keeping that new revelation to herself. Elise felt the weight of everyone's eyes on her and her first instinct was to bury her face in Harris's back, use him as a shield from everyone's curious stares.

"You're that local contractor, right? The one who flips houses?" Regina asked Harris but didn't wait for his response. "You don't know anything about our family, so why don't you stick to hammers and paintbrushes and let me deal with my niece."

The insult may have been directed at Harris, but it crackled through the air like a lightning bolt, shooting Elise into action. Before she could blink, she'd moved in front of him becoming *his* shield.

"How dare you speak to him like that!" Anger vibrated against the back of Elise's throat as she finally unleashed years of words she'd been holding back. "How dare you speak to *anyone* like that? You have always talked down to me, dismissing me and gaslighting me. You made me think that my father had carelessly lost all his money. You made me think that he hadn't had the mental capacity to provide for me. You made me think that he was less than, that *I* was less than, and that both of us should be grateful for your benevolence in taking care of us. Yet the entire time you were treating me as an obligation you could barely tolerate, you were going behind my back and stealing from me. Stealing from my father. If you had only been honest with me, I would've gladly given you some of the money. Lord knows I have more than enough of it. But you lied to me, and you kept me hidden away from anyone who might reveal the truth. And for what? You ended up broke anyway. As soon as my attorney got suspicious and cut you off, you became so desperate that you stole money from a charity. And now you have the audacity to show up tonight, insult everyone else's intelligence by trying to take credit for the event, and then say something so demeaning and dismissive to my boss and friend, as well? You should've just stayed gone. In fact, I suggest you leave again and turn yourself in to the police. They're already looking for you."

When Elise paused long enough to take a breath, she heard a whimpering sound beside her. Pancake was staring up, her big brown eyes filled with concern. She bent down to lift the dog into her arms and when she stood back up, Regina was gone.

And so was Elise's anger. All Elise could feel at that second was relief.

And Harris's hand on her lower back.

"Are you okay?" he murmured softly while forcing a smile toward the onlookers as though nothing was out of the ordinary.

"I think so. If a server passes by, though, I wouldn't mind one of those little avocado toasts. Or a chicken skewer if there's any left. Definitely some scallops. Was that bacon wrapped around them? Why are you looking at me like that?"

Harris's eyes were wide and almost cautious, reminding Elise of when he was trying to hold still so that Oliver the cat would approach. "Because you just told off your aunt in front of all these people, yet you're calm enough to be thinking about food right now."

"To be fair, I've actually been thinking about food for quite some time. Since this afternoon, in fact. But I didn't think it would be too smart to eat anything before the big event in case my stomach got a case of the nerves."

Harris's hand continued to make small circular strokes along her lower back, easing Elise's tension even more. "If you were nervous, nobody could tell once you switched on your mic. Did I mention that you were amazing?"

The compliment immediately went to Elise's head. Or maybe it was the liberating rush of finally confronting Regina once and for all. Of course, it could also be the fact that this dress Roxy had talked her into buying was the nicest and sexiest thing she'd worn since…well since ever. All she knew was that she wanted this well-earned boost of confidence to last as long as possible. And she wanted Harris to look at her with that kind of awe for as long as possible too.

Who knew how long this magical spell might last?

Feeling a boldness she couldn't explain, Elise leaned into Harris's side and whispered in his ear. "You know what sounds better than scallops wrapped in bacon?"

Either she had seduction written all over her face or this wasn't the first time Harris had been propositioned by a woman on a mission. His lids lowered and his nostrils flared ever so slightly.

"Pancakes?" he asked and the puppy in Elise's arms lifted its fuzzy ears upon hearing its name.

Elise laughed. "No, not you, girl. He's talking about the kind with butter and maple syrup. What do you say, Harris? Want to come back to my place for breakfast?"

"Right now?" His brows lifted suggestively. It was barely dinnertime, but they both knew the offer meant he'd stay the night and have pancakes in the morning.

Elise bit her lower lip as she nodded.

"I'll drive," he said, taking her hand and tugging her toward the exit.

Thankfully, Harris had the presence of mind to steer her backstage first to collect her sparkly clutch purse that could barely hold her cell phone, as well as her huge tote bag which held everything else she needed. Unfortunately, they were waylaid by several groups of people who wanted to congratulate Elise on the successful evening, including Doc J.

"This little girl has had a lot of excitement already for one evening," the veterinarian said right before Elise and Harris were about to walk toward the parking lot. Elise blinked several times before realizing he was referring to the sleeping bundle of fur and not to her. "I'll go ahead and take her back now. But if you want to come see her next week, I'd suggest waiting until Tuesday. I just got the cardiologist's report and she's been cleared for her spaying on Monday."

Elise didn't think she could possibly handle any more excitement tonight, but hearing the doctor confirm that Pancake was going to get a second chance at adoption made her so euphoric, she felt as though she was walking on clouds all the way to Harris's truck. Which was saying something since her high heels had started pinching her toes three hours ago.

She slipped them off as soon as she got into the passenger seat and stretched out her feet. When he started the engine, she reached across the console and put her hand on his shoulder. "Are you sure about this?"

Harris threw his head back, his laugh coming out low and throaty. "I feel like I should be asking *you* that question."

"I've never been surer of anything," she confirmed before edging her body over the armrest close enough to kiss him. Just the feel of his warm, full lips against hers made her forget all the stress leading up to today. Harris was the most consistent thing in her life right now, but he was also the most protective. She knew she needed to prove to him, and to herself, that she wasn't some innocent wallflower that had to be sheltered from the messy emotions and complex realities of life.

And if this kiss got any hotter, she'd be proving a lot more of that right there in the Furever Paws parking lot. She reluctantly pulled away, her warm breath panting softy as she tugged at the black silky fabric outlining her breasts. "You might want to drive faster than normal. I'm not used to wearing anything so constricting and I can't wait to get out of this dress."

Harris shifted in his seat and broke several traffic laws as he drove them directly to Maple Street.

Harris awoke the following morning warm, naked and completely satisfied. Elise stretched beside him, the bed sheet slipping low enough that he could see a spot of whisker burn on the smooth curve just below her hardened nipple.

"Good morning," she said, the pink on her cheeks very faint. She hadn't had an ounce of her trademark shyness last night when she'd easily taken charge of their lovemaking. Elise had known exactly what she wanted and exactly how to please him. Now, with the light of day inching through the bedroom windows, Harris could only hope that she wasn't having any regrets.

"Good morning." He smiled, pulling her in closer. She nuzzled her face into his neck, and he inhaled deeply before sighing with relief. "The scent of your shampoo is officially my new favorite smell to wake up to in the morning."

One of her hands rested lazily on his chest. "What was your former favorite smell?"

"Coffee. And bacon. Preferably together."

"I can do both." Elise quickly sprang up to a sitting position, then winced.

Harris immediately lifted his head off the pillow. "Are you okay?"

"I'm fine, it's just that…um…" This time, the blush returned full force and she pulled the sheet higher until it almost reached her collarbone. "I'm not quite used to so much physical activity in the… uh…bedroom and well, I'm a little sore. But you can wipe that look of concern off your face right now, Harris Vega. It was definitely worth it."

If Harris had had better control of himself last night, he would've insisted on slowing things down so they both could take their time. Or maybe stopping after the first two rounds of lovemaking. However, Elise had been so insistent on taking matters into her own hands—both literally and figuratively—and he'd be lying if he said he hadn't enjoyed it.

Harris grinned. "How about you stay here and relax and *I'll* make breakfast?"

Elise tilted her head, causing her loose and somewhat tousled hair to frame her adorable face. "Do you know how to cook?"

"I know how to follow a recipe if there's an online video attached." He winked at her before getting out of bed. "But first, I should probably take a shower."

He padded across the hardwood floors completely naked as though he owned the place. Of course, technically he *did* own it. Until he sold it to Elise. He stood under the steamy water spray thinking back to the day he'd helped Elise change out this very showerhead. The house had come a long way since she'd started cleaning it up and making small touches here and there, but neither one of them had had much time these past few weeks to make any substantial changes. When he'd originally bought it from Mrs. O'Malley, he saw it as an easy flip. The place needed a deep cleaning and some cosmetic upgrades, but it had good bones and was in a prime central neighborhood. Plus, there weren't many lots left in Spring Forest that backed up to a nature preserve with so many beautiful trees and wildlife practically in its backyard.

Buying and selling property was his livelihood, yet for the first time ever, Harris found himself reluctant to sell this particular home.

Home.

All the other places had simply been houses, investments really. They were places for other people—not for him. But something about this little Craftsman on Maple Street felt like an actual home.

Harris shut off the water and grabbed one of the fluffy white towels neatly folded on the shelf. As he dried his face, he inhaled the lingering scent of lavender laundry soap. Yep. Elise had definitely turned this place into a home. One that he wouldn't mind actually living in permanently.

With her.

"Slow it down, hotshot," he told his reflection in the mirror. They'd taken their relationship to the physical level less than twelve hours ago, yet he was already thinking about moving in together. On the other hand, while Harris could be impulsive, he knew that when he had a gut feeling about a good thing, he was rarely wrong. And Elise might be the best thing that had ever happened to him.

He wrapped the towel around his waist and returned to the bedroom to see the bed was already made and his suit was neatly laid out over the dresser. He didn't have to smell the coffee already brewing to know that Elise had beaten him to the kitchen to get breakfast started. Because of course she had. That's what she did. She made things happen behind the scenes.

Behind the scenes. Crap. He'd forgotten about his conversation with Buster last night. He hadn't told Elise about the *Coming Home* article. Grabbing his pants, he decided that it would be best to bring up the subject before she heard about the offer from his foreman. Maybe with the success of last night's fundraiser still on her mind, she might be willing to say yes.

Harris left his shirt and sport coat behind and made his way to the kitchen. "I told you I'd cook breakfast."

Elise turned from the stove and her eyes immediately landed on his bare chest. In fact, she stared so long, Harris thought she might grab his hand and lead him back to the bedroom, like she'd done last night. Finally, she licked her lips then said, "You can't cook bacon shirtless. You'll get burned by the grease splatters."

"It's worth the risk," he said, coming to stand behind her and putting his arms around her waist. Just as she began to ease back against him, he heard a pop and then felt a burning sting from a splatter hitting his forearm. "Damn. Maybe I'll just work on the pancake batter instead."

Elise chuckled and watched as he helplessly opened and closed cabinet doors looking for ingredients and mixing bowls. As she stood guard over the bacon, she took pity on him, talking him through the steps of combining the flour and baking soda. She even left the skillet unattended long enough to help him dig several pieces of shell out of the mix after he cracked an egg too hard.

"We make a pretty good team, you know," Harris started as he whisked in the buttermilk. "Both at work and here at home. I mean, at *your* home, but also at other homes. Or anywhere really."

He dared a quick glance at her face to see if she'd caught his slip. She stared intently at the bacon, so maybe he'd done a decent job at playing it off and not sounding like he was already asking to move in together. "Anyway, speaking of teams and partnerships, I got a call from the editor at *Coming Home* yesterday. They're interested in doing an entire issue on remodeled colonials and found out about the work we're doing on Dawson Avenue. They want to give us the magazine cover and a ten-page spread."

Elise removed the bacon from the skillet and then turned off the burner. "Us? You mean you and Buster and the rest of the crew?"

She didn't look in his direction or even shift positions. She just kind of stood there staring at the plate of sizzling bacon, a pair of tongs still clutched in her hand.

"Well, yeah, the guys will likely be in some of the shots and have their names mentioned, but the editor was pretty clear that the feature focus of the article would be the design process." Harris massaged her shoulder lightly, easing her to face him. "And *you're* the designer, Elise."

"So they'd want to what? Interview me?"

"Yes, but we could do the interview together. We have plenty of 'before' pictures from the real estate listing and Buster always snaps photos on his phone during the demo because, well, that's his favorite part of the job. But they're going to send a photographer out next week to get some working shots and then come again once the remodel is complete for the 'after' pics. The editor said they always like to include pictures with the owners and the designers to bring it all to life. Personally, I'm not into all the fanfare and attention, but it is a pretty big honor to be selected. It would be a huge boost for the launch of Elise Mackenzie Interiors."

She sighed and shook her head. "But they're not interested in the house because of *me*. They've never even heard of me. It's Harris Vega, one of the Top Thirty Under Thirty, they want. I'd just be riding your coattails."

"So then ride them. You know how many people in this industry would kill for an opportunity like this?"

"But I haven't earned it, at least not yet. I need to stop depending on other people and start standing on my own. I don't even know who Elise Mackenzie *is*, let alone what Elise Mackenzie Interiors is. Or what I want it to be." She pointed the tongs right at him. "Hell, it's not even a real business. It's just an idea you came up with to help give me some direction in life and to ease the guilt of crossing professional boundaries."

This wasn't going exactly how he thought it would. He crossed his arms over his chest. "I thought you liked designing."

"I do. But I also like cooking. You didn't suggest I open a restaurant, though, Harris. You came up with a business model for *me* that would ultimately benefit *you*."

Damn.

Her accusation hit the mark and the verbal blow was strong enough to make him physically take a step back as her words ricocheted inside his head. Did she seriously think he was using her for his own benefit?

"Elise, I don't care what you do in the future—"

Her apron pocket rang before he could finish telling her that all he cared about was that her future included him in it.

Elise pulled out the phone and the color drained from her face. Her fingers began to tremble as she stared at the mobile device. "It's the county sheriff."

The last thing Harris should do at that second was try to take control of the situation—especially after her impassioned speech about standing on her own. Yet he couldn't stop himself from wanting to help her. "Do you want me to answer it?"

Elise bit her lower lip, then shook her head as she stared at the screen. "No, I'll do it. But maybe you could just…"

She let the request hang in the air and Harris didn't know whether she wanted him to stay or to go. But when she answered the call on speakerphone, he couldn't help but think she must want him there.

The automated greeting informed them that the call was being placed from a detention facility and would possibly be recorded. Then her aunt's name in an electronic, yet still haughty, voice was identified as the inmate placing the call.

Elise tapped the number to accept and immediately Regina Mackenzie was live on the other end of the line.

"Elise? It's your aunt Regina. I'm calling you from jail."

"Yes, I inferred that from the caller ID and from the recording saying you were an inmate at a detention facility."

Regina must have missed her niece's sarcasm because the woman continued talking. "Those crazy Whitaker sisters had me arrested in the middle of the night."

"I hate to break it to you, Regina, but the Whitaker sisters aren't the only people filing criminal charges against you."

Again, Regina ignored her niece, likely the same way she had the past several years. "I hadn't even gotten the suitcase in my car when the cops showed up in my driveway. They accused me of trying to abscond from the law. As if I was some sort of common criminal. I explained that I wasn't *leaving*, leaving. I was simply going to visit one of my friends in South America. But because of the police and their tacky handcuffs, I've now missed my flight. My attorney isn't answering his phone and the public defender they assigned me says that the judge at my bail hearing this morning might frown upon my travel itinerary. Anyway, I need you to call Les Rocklin. He's supposedly the best defense attorney in town, which is why you'll have to pay him his retainer in advance. Then I need you to go to the station and explain that this is all a big misunderstanding. Detective Sorrento says she's already talked to you, so you should be able to work things out. Then bring me my pale blue Armani suit and my Jimmy Choos with the three inch heel. Not the brown ones, the beige ones. They took all of my personal belongings and issued me this ridiculous bright orange jumpsuit when it's clear that I'm a winter color palette—"

"Regina." Elise had to raise her voice to finally get her aunt to stop talking. "I am not hiring an attorney for you. And even if the judge determines that you're not a flight risk, I'm not bailing you out of jail. I'm also not telling the detectives this was a misunderstanding and I'm most definitely not bringing you any damn clothes. Perhaps I didn't make myself clear last night when I said that I wanted you to stay away from me."

Harris nodded and would've pumped his fist in support, but he didn't want to distract Elise. Besides, she was clearly doing just fine all on her own.

"How could you do this to me, young lady?" Regina's tone was not only accusatory, it was nearly threatening. "I'm family. I took care of you when nobody else would."

"You were paid to do that. Or did you forget how much you benefited financially from having me around?"

Okay, so Harris didn't exactly like her use of the word *benefited* since it was the same thing she'd accused him of moments ago. She didn't consider him to be the same as Regina, did she?

"Oh, spare me, kid. You were so naive and socially awkward, you would've thrown all that wealth away at the first guy who came sniffing around. I was protecting you from money-grubbers like that contractor you were cozying up to last night. You called him your boss, right? I bet he was real quick to hire you after he found out what an easy mark you were."

Elise's knuckles turned white as she clenched the phone tighter. "Harris is my friend. He gave me a place to live when my so-called protective aunt took off with all my money and left me broke with no means to support myself."

Ouch. The word *friend* stung him just as much as the word *benefited*. Worse, maybe because he'd been hoping Elise saw him as more than that after last night.

"So is he your boss or is he your landlord? Please don't tell me he's both. You're clearly just another one of his fixer-upper projects. You may have gotten a makeover and looked like the belle of the ball last night, but that man will soon grow bored and move on, just like he does every time he sells another house. There's no way you were foolish enough to give some random guy that much power over you."

"I was foolish enough to trust *you*," Elise shot back at her aunt. "You didn't protect me. You purposely isolated me to keep me and my inheritance under your control. How could you lie to me? More importantly, how could you lie about my father? It was bad enough that he had to suffer the indignity of Alzheimer's, but you let me believe that he failed me."

The automated voice clicked onto the line before Regina could come up with another deflection. "You have one minute remaining."

"I don't need another minute. I've said all I needed to say." Elise hit the red button on her phone and disconnected the call.

Harris stood there, his hands hanging uselessly at his side as the silence between them filled the kitchen. While he was filled with pride that Elise had stood her ground with her aunt, his chest also felt a weird sort of emptiness at hearing Regina say such awful things about him.

Scratch that. He wasn't hurt by Regina's words. She was a spiteful person whose opinion meant absolutely nothing to him. His emptiness came from Elise not defending him. He'd thought he'd meant more to her than just a boss or a landlord or even a friend.

"I'm sorry you had to hear that," Elise finally said.

"I'm sorry you had to *live* with that." As unsettled as Harris felt right at that second, he knew Elise had to be reeling inside. It was selfish of him to be thinking about himself. He looked at the cold bacon and the abandoned pancake batter. If he stayed for breakfast, he knew that he wouldn't be able to pretend that the phone call hadn't happened.

He couldn't erase all the cruel words said in the past few minutes or all the financial and emotional damage done these past few years. This was one problem Harris Vega couldn't fix. But he could give Elise the thing she'd asked for earlier.

Time.

He reached up to cup the side of her face until she was looking directly at him. "Listen, when you and I were talking right before your aunt interrupted us, I think you made a valid point about wanting to stand on your own and figure out who you are. I know that I'm not the man Regina is accusing me of being, and as much as I want to prove that to you, I also want to give you the space you need to come to your own conclusions. Remember when I told you about my family motto applying to the big decisions? Well, this is the biggest one I've ever made. I'm willing to take the chance, but only if you're willing to take it with me. So when you're ready to talk, you know where to find me."

Elise's eyes searched his face and it took every drop of willpower he possessed not to yank her into his arms and hold on to her for all he was worth. Instead, he brushed his lips against hers and then walked away.

Chapter Fourteen

Elise stood in front of her stove, doing what she always did when she couldn't think of what to do. She cooked. Then she cleaned. Then she cooked some more. But there was only so much stuff she could do around the house to keep her mind occupied.

Making love to Harris had changed everything.

Then he shocked her the following morning with that comment about them making a good team at work and at home. He'd tried to play it off, but Harris had already proven himself to be impulsive and protective and almost overcharitable in everything he did. How could Elise trust that he wasn't going to say or commit to something that he'd regret later? Or trust herself not to be so desperate and naive that she'd believe anything he had to say, throwing herself into a relationship without stopping to consider whether it was built to last?

When she'd told him that she didn't know who she was, it might've been a bit too defensive. But it was also true. Elise *was* still finding out what she wanted to do with her life and if she even wanted her own business. What she didn't get a chance to tell him, though, was that she was enjoying the discovery process with Harris by her side.

She'd said she didn't want to be dependent on anyone, but really had she ever been that dependent on Regina? Emotionally, Elise had been on her own since her dad had gone into assisted living. Financially, she'd thought she had to rely on her aunt because she had no resources of her own, but that had proven to be a lie. Elise had now proven to herself that she could pay her own way, even before she'd found out about her inheritance. Sure she'd lived paycheck to paycheck and had to be frugal, but she'd done it.

If she wanted to be with Harris, though, she would have to allow herself to become emotionally vulnerable. She thought she'd been brave when she'd struck out on her own to find a place to live, a job, a lifestyle that she could afford. But this was much, much scarier. How did one open up to needing someone else without getting hurt? Especially when her trust had just recently been betrayed? That was what she hadn't figured out yet. Was it even possible for someone like her to open herself up to that? She wasn't like the rest of the Vega family. She didn't take chances.

When Harris brought up the magazine article, Elise really began to question herself. By the time Regina had called with her ridiculous demands and manipulative accusations, the seeds of doubt had already been planted. Elise didn't blame Harris for being insulted or for leaving. What surprised her, though, was to hear him say he was going to give her space to figure things out on her own.

That had been two days ago, and she still hadn't heard from him.

All she could think of was that time with the feral cat colony when they were trying to catch Oliver, the orange tabby cat. Harris told Elise that he always went after what he wanted. Since he'd stayed away this long, did that mean he didn't want her? Or was he really doing the honorable thing and waiting her out like he thought she wanted? The same way she'd insisted they wait out Oliver?

Elise opened the fridge and closed it, realizing there wasn't an inch of room left inside for any more pre-prepped meals. The floors had been scrubbed—twice—and the laundry was all washed and put away. With the fundraiser over, the last thing left for her to focus her energy on was design work. But that only made her think more about Harris, who might not be thinking about her at all.

Ugh. All this quiet was driving her crazy. Maybe she should go for a walk. Elise grabbed her sneakers and the spare leash she now kept for Mr. Frankfurter whenever he would scratch at her back door. She went across the street to Roxy's house, but nobody was home. Looking at her watch, she realized that the afternoon training classes would be starting soon at Barkyard. She couldn't show up during the middle of a session and distract the students. Elise was determined to walk a dog, yet she didn't have a single dog to walk.

Furever Paws was the next logical choice, even though Bethany had told her that most of the pets had been adopted after the fundraiser and they were waiting for new ones to arrive. Maybe she could feed the farm animals or clean reptile cages.

She needed something to focus her energy on and it was either that or drive to the Vega Homes office and warehouse to catalogue the contents of the staging furniture. Harris should be at the jobsite today supervising the concrete slab pour for the new front porch. Elise hoped he remembered that she wanted to do an exposed aggregate finish with a blue-tinted color seal. Maybe she should drive over there quickly and remind him.

No. If Harris was going to give *her* space, then she was going to give him space, as well.

She got in her car and went straight to the animal shelter instead. She would walk as many potbellied pigs and goats as she could to prove to herself that she could live without one particular man.

When Elise parked at the side of the building, Birdie Whitaker was outside with Pancake, who was wearing a plastic cone and refusing to walk on her leash. The puppy yipped with excitement when she saw Elise and made a small piddle before forgetting about the awkward cone and rolling onto her back to expose her tummy for a rub.

Elise knelt to pet the happy pup, being careful to avoid the fresh stitches. "Hi, girl. How did the big surgery go yesterday?"

"Doc J said she did great. We're seeing how she does on her antibiotics the next twenty-four hours, but if her vitals all stay good, she'll be ready for adoption." Birdie studied Elise. "You know, we already have a wait list of applicants. Probably because that fellow of yours carried her around all night showing her off to everyone at the fundraiser."

"Harris? He isn't my fellow," Elise said, while navigating the mixed emotions of being happy for Pancake and also a little bit jealous that someone else would get to take the sweet girl home.

"Sure he's not." Birdie added to her obvious sarcasm with an exaggerated wink. "Just like lil' Pancake here isn't yours either."

Elise looked down at her hand, not sure when

she'd taken the leash from the older woman. It had been so natural. The puppy was also willingly walking now that her preferred person was in charge.

This wasn't good.

Defensiveness crept back into Elise's voice. "Oh, I don't know that I'm the right person to be adopting a dog. If you want to know the truth, I'm a little bit of a stray myself."

Birdie just flicked her age-spotted wrist dismissively. "Oh, honey, strays need someone to love them too. Even those feral cats you're feeding for Mrs. O'Malley can't be on their own *all* the time. Every creature on earth eventually has to learn to trust something."

Elise sighed. "But after everything with my aunt, it might take a bit more than some Feline Finest to get me to start trusting again."

"Speaking of your aunt, I should probably tell you that Bunny and I talked it over, and we decided to drop the charges against her."

For a moment, Elise could only stare in shock. "B-but," she stammered, "she stole money from a charity. How can you forgive a person who would do something like that?"

"Because it all worked out in the end and the shelter raised more money with you leading the charge than it ever would have if she hadn't left town. Besides, I have known Regina Mackenzie for as long as I can remember. I'll never forget tenth grade when she and I had to sew matching dresses for our final grade in home ec. I had zero fashion sense back then, too, and she came up with the design and ended up doing all the work for both of us. Anyway, I'm sure you have some good memories of her, as well. She wasn't always so unscrupulous, she just got caught up in her lifestyle and let the money and appearances go to her head. The same thing happened with my brother Gator a few years back. Now I'm not saying that you need to forgive your aunt. Everyone's been talking about what you said to her at the fundraiser. It's obvious she took way bigger advantage of you than she did with Furever Paws. But holding on to the hurt isn't going to make you feel any better."

Elise lifted her head to the sky and took a deep breath. "You're right. There were some good memories mixed in there, way back when. After my mom died, she convinced my dad that I still needed a woman's influence, and she would take me on what she called *girl days*. The shopping trips for clothes were awful, but I used to actually enjoy it when we'd go to different furniture stores and she'd ask me my opinion on fabrics and styles. The best times, though, were when we'd drive to the Outer Banks and spend the day at the beach. Regina was always so much more mellow away from town and her self-imposed social constraints. Once, as we were driving home from one of those trips, she told me about the child she'd miscarried, and I remember thinking that was why she was always throwing parties and buying herself new things. She needed something to make herself happy."

Birdie nodded. "Some people fill the emotional voids in their life with parties and some people fill it with other things, like dedicating their lives to caring for animals in need. Man, I'm going to miss this place like crazy when I go next month."

Go? Birdie Whitaker would never willingly leave Spring Forest unless—Elise gasped at the realization. "I'm so sorry. I didn't know you were having health issues."

"Oh, no, I don't mean I'm going in *that* sense. I'm just moving to Florida with Doc J." Birdie held up her left hand to show a simple, yet elegant engagement ring. "We're getting married and, like he promised me, there's plenty of animals in Florida that need rescuing too."

"Oh, that's wonderful. Congratulations. But what about Bunny?" The previously single sisters had been living together on their family's property forever. It was rare to see one without seeing the other.

"Stew is going to finally sell that RV of his and buy out my share of Whitaker Acres. See, it's not just you. Even a couple of old spinsters like us apparently need someone to love. Anyway, Stew and Bunny are looking at smaller camper vans, though, because they'll obviously want to drive down to

Florida to visit. What do Harris's parents think of their travel trailer?"

Elise spoke to Birdie for a few minutes longer as Pancake walked slowly around the dog run to get some post-surgery exercise. When the puppy stopped in her tracks and laid down at Elise's feet, there was no question that it was nap time.

"Poor thing is exhausted already," Birdie said sympathetically. "The pain meds make her even sleepier than normal."

"I guess I better say goodbye so she can go back inside and rest." Elise turned over the leash to Birdie and knelt to give Pancake one last pet and a kiss on top of her soft head. The clearly fatigued pooch whimpered in response. "I know, girl. But it's for your own good. Sometimes we need a break, even from the people we love, so that we can recharge our batteries."

Oh no.

That's why this forced separation had been so frustrating. Elise loved Harris.

And why wouldn't she? He had never asked her to be anything but herself—or at least a better, truer version of herself. He'd encouraged her independence, but had also accepted her shyness. He was everything Elise would have wanted in a man if she'd been looking for one. Which she clearly hadn't been.

Like Birdie said, though, even strays needed to be able to trust someone.

Elise had always been too shy, too nervous, too comfortable with the status quo to recognize her own loneliness before. But she couldn't keep going through life unsure of herself and letting others make decisions for her. That's how she'd ended up with Regina taking control of everything.

But no more.

As much as Elise thought she needed time to sort things out for herself, she also needed to take charge of her life and make a decision rather than waiting for everything to fall into place on its own. And taking charge meant no longer being indecisive or allowing Harris to call the shots on how much space she needed.

She followed Birdie and Pancake inside Furever Paws and then later that night she sent a text to Harris asking him if he was still planning to drop off the weekly order of Feline Finest tomorrow.

Harris walked up to the back porch of the Maple Street house on Wednesday morning with a twenty-pound bag of kibble in one arm and a pair of black satin high heels in his free hand. Elise's text had asked him to come before work, but he was an hour early.

Before he could knock, Elise opened the door holding a plate stacked high with pancakes and wearing her hair loose around her face. Just like it had been a few mornings ago. After they'd made love.

Lord, a man could get used to coming home to this sight.

Harris had to school his features and rein in his thoughts. It had nearly killed him to stay away from her these past three days. To not even text her a picture of the new concrete patio slab at the Dawson Avenue project and tell her that she'd been right and the aggregate finish made it sparkle in the sun. So when he saw her message about bringing more Feline Finest, it was all he could do not to drive it over that very night.

"Hey. I hope I'm not too early." He tried for the most casual expression he could manage with his jaw clenching and his heart racing.

Elise smiled. "I had a feeling you wouldn't be able to wait until eight o'clock." Her eyes dropped to the shoes he was holding. "Are those mine?"

"Yeah. I've been driving around with them in my truck since the night of the fundraiser when I brought you home."

"I didn't even realize they were missing. I would've been happy to come pick them up if you'd told me I left them."

"Nope. I was trying to be a man of my word and give you your space. I knew that if I so much as sent you a text, I'd end up professing my love and trying to convince you to be more than business partners."

Elise bit her lower lip, but this time the twinkle in her eyes seemed more calculating than nervous. "How much more?"

The words he'd been holding back for a while now tumbled out of his mouth before he could stop them. "I'd prefer the husband-and-wife kind of partnership, but I'll take anything I can get at this point."

"Is this you taking your chance?" The corner of Elise's mouth lifted in a smirk.

"I already took that chance once I realized the odds were in my favor. I may seem impulsive at times, but I also know a good thing when I see it. And you, Elise Mackenzie, are the best thing I've ever known. I love you and I'll wait for as long as it takes for you to realize that you love me, as well."

"Then I better not keep you waiting any longer. I love you, too, Harris." Her words sent tremors through his muscles until all the tension of the past few days vanished. He dropped the sack of cat food next to his boots, ready to lift her off her feet and spin her around. But she held up her palm. "First, though, I have a list of conditions before we can begin any sort of partnership."

Harris smiled, his heart suddenly open to any and all negotiations. "You know how much I love your lists."

Elise narrowed her eyes playfully. "Number one, you let me buy half of this house from you."

"Agreed, as long as I can move into it with you and have some say in the remodel and design. Especially anything that has to do with the plumbing."

"Fair enough. Number two." She pulled a set of keys out of her pocket. "You let me drive when we take the Scout to be reunited with its rightful owner."

Harris's eyes followed her mischievous gaze to the restored yellow 4x4 parked on the other side of the shed and his jaw dropped. "How did you…? Where did…? I thought your aunt sold all of them."

"The attorney told me several of Dad's prized cars were tied up in the trust and there were specific directions from my father that I oversee this one's return to his friend, Simon Vega."

Emotion swelled in Harris's throat and he had to swallow several times before he could speak. "I can't even think about what this is going to mean to my dad, let alone talk about it right now."

Elise's smile was tender and full of understanding. "I had the exact same response when I saw it on the inventory list."

He blinked his eyes a few times to clear away the dampness. "Well." He huffed out a breath. "We better get back to your list."

"Number three, you let me do most of the cooking." At his frown, Elise quickly explained. "I saw your egg cracking skills the other day and Buster is more delicate in a kitchen than you."

"I will gladly let you do all of the cooking *in* the house. But you have to agree to let me take you out to dinner when we get extra busy at work and I'm craving a bacon cheeseburger." He pulled Elise into his arms, careful not to tip the full plate still balanced in her hand. "Although, I promise that I'll always be in the mood for your pancakes."

"Funny you should mention that since I have a fourth condition."

"Oh yeah?" He kissed the tip of her nose. "What's number four?"

"I hope you love *all* the pancakes in this house." She took a step back and set the plate on the entry table. Then she pushed the door open wider to reveal a sleeping puppy curled up in a dog bed in the corner of the kitchen. "Because I just signed the adoption papers last night and now we're a package deal."

Harris's burst of laughter woke up the sleeping dog, who blinked twice before recognizing him and ambling over awkwardly with her little cone around her neck.

"I can't believe you beat me to it again," he said to Elise as he lowered himself to the floor so that the fluffy golden retriever, who was still obviously on pain meds, could climb onto his lap. "First the feral cats and now this. The morning I drove away from here, I called Bunny Whitaker to put my name on the top of the wait list to adopt Pancake. I mean, I know I promised to wait until you came to your own conclusions about me, but I had every intention of hedging my bets. After all, you might not say yes to an engagement ring right away, but there was no way you'd turn down a proposal with a puppy you were already half in love with."

"You have got to be the most confident person I know, Harris Vega." Elise rolled her eyes but was also chuckling as she joined him and the dog on the ground. "I guess this is what you meant when you told me that you always go after what you want."

"This is exactly what I meant." He wrapped an arm around her shoulders and pulled her in for a deep kiss. "And right now, there is nothing I want more than to hear you tell me again that you love me."

"I love you. And I love who I am when I'm with you. I've never been more ready to officially get this partnership started."

Pancake, who was now wide awake and jumping from Harris's lap to Elise's, gave an enthusiastic bark in agreement.

* * * * *

*Catch up with the previous stories in the
Furever Yours series*

Look for

Home is Where the Hound Is
by Melissa Senate

More Than a Temporary Family
by USA TODAY *bestselling author*
Marie Ferrarella

The Bookshop Rescue
by Rochelle Alers

Love Off the Leash
by USA TODAY *bestselling author*
Tara Taylor Quinn

A Double Dose of Happiness
by USA TODAY *bestselling author Teri Wilson*

*Available now, wherever Harlequin Special Edition
books and ebooks are sold.*

SPECIAL EXCERPT FROM

HARLEQUIN
SPECIAL EDITION

*Single mom Cierra Greene is determined to succeed
in real estate. Too bad her most lucrative property for
sale is...haunted? Reluctantly, she seeks out Wesley
Livingston, the cohost of a popular paranormal
investigation show, for help. Cierra and Wesley try to
ignore their unfinished business, but when old feelings
resurface, things get complicated...*

Read on for a sneak peek at
The Spirit of Second Chances,
*the latest book in Synithia Williams's
Heart & Soul miniseries!*

Cierra's lips lifted in a smile that brightened his dark
corner of the coffee shop as she straightened. "Oh, good,
you remember me," she said, as if he could possibly
forget her.

How could he forget Cierra Greene? Head cheerleader,
class president, most popular girl in school and slayer of
teenage boys' hearts.

"Yeah...I remember you." He managed to keep his
voice calm even though his heart thumped as if he'd had
a dozen cappuccinos.

"I was worried because you didn't return any of my
calls." She tilted her head to the side and her thick, dark
hair shifted. Her smile didn't go away, but there was the
barest hint of accusation in her voice.

Wesley shifted in his seat. He hadn't returned her
calls because ever since the day Cierra told him after a

basketball game that she was ditching him for his former best friend, he'd vowed to never speak to her again. He realized vows made in high school didn't have to follow him into adulthood, but the moment he'd heard her voice message saying she'd like to meet up and talk, he'd deleted it and tried to move on with his life.

"I've been busy," he said.

"Good thing I caught you here, then, huh?" She moved to the opposite side of the table and pulled out the other chair and sat.

"How did you know I was here?"

"Mrs. Montgomery," she said, as if he should have known that one of the most respected women in town would give his whereabouts to her. She must have read the confusion on his face because she laughed, that lighthearted laugh that, unfortunately, still made his heart skip a beat. "When I couldn't reach you, my mom called around. Mrs. Montgomery said you typically spend Friday afternoons here. So, here I am!" She held out her arms and spoke as if she were a present.

Her bright smile and enthusiasm stunned him for a second. Wesley cleared his throat and took a sip of his coffee to compose himself. How many years later—fifteen—and he still had the lingering remnants of a crush on her?

Come on, Wes, you gotta do better than that!

He took a long breath and looked back at her. "Here you are."

Get 4 FREE REWARDS!

We'll send you 2 FREE Books plus 2 FREE Mystery Gifts.

FREE
Value Over
$20

Both the **Harlequin® Special Edition** and **Harlequin® Heartwarming™** series feature compelling novels filled with stories of love and strength where the bonds of friendship, family and community unite.

HARLEQUIN
PLUS

Announcing a **BRAND-NEW** multimedia subscription service for romance fans like you!

Read, Watch and Play.

Experience the easiest way to get the romance content you crave.

Start your **FREE 7 DAY TRIAL** at <u>www.harlequinplus.com/freetrial</u>.

HARLEQUIN

Heartfelt or thrilling, passionate or uplifting—Harlequin is more than just happily-ever-after.

With twelve different series to choose from and new books available every month, you are sure to find stories that will move you, uplift you, inspire and delight you.

Love Harlequin romance?

DISCOVER.

Be the first to find out about promotions,
news and exclusive content!

f Facebook.com/HarlequinBooks

🐦 Twitter.com/HarlequinBooks

📷 Instagram.com/HarlequinBooks

📌 Pinterest.com/HarlequinBooks

You Tube YouTube.com/HarlequinBooks

ReaderService.com

EXPLORE.

Sign up for the Harlequin e-newsletter and
download a free book from any series at
TryHarlequin.com

CONNECT.

Join our Harlequin community to
share your thoughts and connect
with other romance readers!
Facebook.com/groups/HarlequinConnection

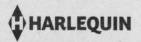